Praise for **paper aeroplanes** by Dawn O'Porter

'*Paper Aeroplanes* is one of the best debut novels I've read. Teenage friendships are very potent and O'Porter captures that.' Alex Jones, *Mail on Sunday*

'O'Porter perfectly captures the sometimes ludicrous complexities of adolescence, and everyone should relate to this heartbreakingly funny depiction of friendship and loss.' *The Irish Times*

'Set in the mid-1990s and based loosely on her own experiences, TV presenter and journalist Dawn O'Porter's first novel is a tale of two unlikely friends who find common ground in their dysfunctional families. Funny, touching and packed with cultural references, this is a must for anyone who has experienced the joy – and pain – of teenage friendship.' *Grazia*

'A cringingly honest account of teenage friendship in the 1990s ... a really gorgeous and nostalgic read.' *Marie Claire*

goose

goose

DAWN O'PORTER

HOT
KEY
BOOKS

First published in Great Britain in 2014 by Hot Key Books
Northburgh House, 10 Northburgh Street, London EC1V 0AT

A CIP catalogue record for this book is available from the British Library.

ISBN: 978-1-4714-0063-6

1

This book is typeset in 10.5 Berling LT Std using Atomik ePublisher

Printed and bound by Clays Ltd, St Ives Plc

FSC

Hot Key Books supports the Forest Stewardship Council (FSC),
the leading international forest certification organisation, and is
committed to printing only on Greenpeace-approved FSC-certified paper.

www.hotkeybooks.com

Hot Key Books is part of the Bonnier Publishing Group
www.bonnierpublishing.com

For Louise and Carrie, my girls x

'Are you sure you're ready to get rid of it?' I say to Aunty Jo as she drives us towards town.

'Never more certain about a thing,' she says.

We pull up outside the house and it's very obvious that there's no one home. He is probably in the pub, like he always is on a Friday night.

'OK, let's do this,' I say.

We get out and drag Ricky out of the boot. Still looking ravishing in Aunty Jo's wedding dress, we tiptoe him to the front door. As I open a wheelie bin, Aunty Jo tips him in.

'Leave his feet poking out,' I say. Aunty Jo closes the lid, making sure that two bony feet hang out over the top.

'OK, quick. Let's go,' she says.

We jump back in the car and spin off. Aunty Jo stops at the first phone box we see.

'Off you go then. Go and do the deed.'

I dial 999.

'Hello. Police, please. Yes, I'd like to report some suspicious activity. I just saw a grown man throw a human skeleton into a wheelie bin.'

Guernsey

April 1997

1

Never Give Up on the Good Times

Renée

'Don't spend all that lunch money on sausage rolls!' yells Aunty Jo as I leave the house and walk to my car, my jacket hanging over my right shoulder. My hair is wet, my toothbrush is hanging out of my mouth and I'm holding my skirt up with my hand because I didn't have time to zip it up properly. My other hand is holding my car keys, my bag and a strawberry Pop Tart. As usual, I am really late for school.

I open the door of my Fiat 126 and throw everything except my toothbrush onto the passenger seat. Then, still holding up my unzipped skirt, I open the boot and pour into the engine the contents of the bottle of green anti-freeze that I left under my back wheel when I got home last night. When the bottle is empty I slam the boot shut, spit toothpaste into the hedge, get into my car, push in my Spice Girls tape and set off for school. It's a lovely sunny April day.

I got my car for twenty-five quid off a friend of Aunty Jo's who won the local lottery and bought a BMW. If I won the lottery I would probably buy a BMW too, but there is no way I would sell my Fiat. It's falling apart, the brakes barely work so I have to slow down using my gears, and when it's cold I have to make sure I park on a hill so I can jump-start it. But I love that car with all my heart. It's so cute and teeny-tiny. Smaller than a Mini. I did once get six people in it from school, though, and drove us all to town. I had a foot in my face the whole way, but it was fun. And that is what I love about my little car: it's funny. It makes people laugh. Anyone who gets in it knows they are going to have a good time. It's fast too – I reached 55mph on the coast road last week. And even though it pumps out green anti-freeze and needs refilling every twenty minutes, you can actually get a long way on the island of Guernsey in that time.

When I arrive at school the car park is full, but as usual my best friend Flo has parked her car slightly over the line so that only my teeny-tiny one can fit in the space next to it. I park up and adjust my rear-view mirror so I can see my face. I scramble around in my glove box to find some black eye liner, draw once around both eyes, tie my hair into a pony tail, zip up my bag and get out.

I shudder as I walk past Flo's car. It's her brother Julian's old car, the same car I lost my virginity to him in two years ago. I've been in the car since then – Flo learned to drive a few months before me so she'd pick me up in it, but it always feels awkward, because what happened between me and Julian nearly split

6

me and Flo up. Sleeping with – and I'm sure that expression was invented by parents so they never have to actually use the word sex – Flo's brother is the stupidest thing I have ever done, and even though she has forgiven me for it we don't talk about my virginity because it involved me lying to Flo and really hurting her. It's the elephant in the room. Though at the time it felt like there was an elephant in my pants.

Flo

I don't like being in the common room on my own. It's really intimidating. Renée and I only joined the grammar school last year, and the girls who were already here gave us a bit of a hard time at the beginning. I think they felt like they owned the boys in their year and then we came along and the boys were interested to see what we were all about. It is better now than it was in the Lower Sixth, but when I am in the common room on my own I still feel like they're all making spastic faces behind my back because they know that I'm a virgin.

'How late am I?' says Renée, making her usual grand entrance as she kicks the door open. She drops her bag on the floor and gives me a hug. 'Thanks for saving me my spot.'

I hug her back. 'Thank God you're here. This room gives me the fear so badly.'

Renée's eyes narrow. 'Has someone said something to you? Who? What did they say?' She jumps into a ninja pose.

We both laugh. Sometimes I wonder if Renée actually enjoys people picking on me so she can stick up for me and have a go at them. She's all about being the protective best friend.

We had to really stick together when we first started here. We felt like we were lost among the huge number of people in our year. At Tudor Falls School for Girls there were only thirty-five of us – here there are nearly 150. At first we were in our little bubble, just so happy to be together that we barely noticed anyone else, but when we did, it felt a bit overwhelming.

'No,' I say. 'No one said anything. But that doesn't stop me thinking they do, does it?'

'You're so paranoid, Flo,' Renée says, ruffling my hair like I am a little child. 'How many times do I have to tell you that you have me now. Who cares what anyone else thinks?'

I get my books out of my locker and smile. She's right, I shouldn't care. But I am plagued with insecurity. It was drummed into me over years of being teased by Sally de Putron that I'm square and not good enough. Sally might not be around me any more, but the constant jibing I had from her means that I presume the worst of people's feelings towards me at all times. Life would be much easier if I was more like Renée. Having said that, she *does* care about what people think of her – she is just better at hiding it.

'I can't believe the exams start in six weeks,' I say to Renée. 'It feels like ages since we filled out our UCAS forms. I remember watching you walk away to the post office thinking we had years until we had to think about A levels and here we are, about to do them. I really hope we both go to Nottingham. It looks fun there. Me at the uni, you at the polytechnic . . . That worked out really well, you still being able to do English even though you failed so many GCSEs . . . Renée?' I nudge her. 'Renée, are you listening? Are you getting excited about going to Nottingham?'

'Urgh,' Renée sighs. 'I don't know. I only applied to do English so I can read books, but there is so much writing you have to do. The idea of writing even more essays when I leave here is not how I want to spend my first few years of freedom . . . ' She shakes her head. 'I dunno. I've gone off the idea, to be honest.'

I stare at my best friend, confused. 'Gone off the idea? You mean you don't want to do English? Maybe you could swap courses. I'm sure if you call them and explain you've had a change of heart they might consider you for something else. What about Classics? Or Cookery? You love food.'

'It's not the course, it's going on to study at all. I just don't think I want to spend another three years doing schoolwork.'

I feel panicky. 'But . . . what about us, Renée? What about our plan? That we would go somewhere where I could go to the uni, you could go to the poly, and we would be in the same city so we could live with each other and go away together?'

'I just don't think we should worry about what each other does. We should just do what we want,' she says, resiliently.

I watch her stuff clothes and packets of crisps into her locker and then try to push the door shut with her shoulder. She doesn't seem at all fazed by what she has just said. I feel a tingling in my nose, which means I am going to cry. Please, no.

'You mean you don't want to go to uni with me, like we said?' I ask, my voice unnecessarily high pitched.

'No, I don't mean that. I just mean if it doesn't work out then we shouldn't let it stop us doing what we want to do.

We can still see each other, go stay with each other, plan good weekends, that sort of thing. Just don't worry about it. You've been waiting to get off Guernsey most of your life – you can't let my choices hold you back from going where you want to go,' Renée says, like the thought of us splitting up isn't hideously awful.

'Don't worry, I won't,' I say. Hurt, and with a nose full of that annoying runny snot that comes with tears. I manage to sniff it all back up, which sounds disgusting and makes me feel embarrassed. 'It doesn't matter.'

Renée grabs my arm and smiles. 'It really doesn't. We'll work it out. Come on, I'll walk you to your RS lesson. I've got Classical Civilisation. Because learning about gods from a billion years ago who probably didn't even exist is just what every girl needs to arm her against the challenges of the modern world!'

We walk together down the corridor. Renée talks about what she plans to have for lunch and she doesn't seem to notice that I say nothing at all.

I feel nervous, and like everything is about to change.

Renée

I walk Flo to her RS class, arrange to go over to hers later on and then amble casually to the Classics room.

I already know I will probably fail Classical Civilisation, as I have only been to about ten of the classes this year. It's so incredibly boring, and it is so easy to skive at the grammar school. At Tudor Falls avoiding detentions wasn't easy. I bunked off loads of lessons and got into trouble a lot, that was just that. But here, all we have to do is sign out. There's a big registration book by the school entrance where you write your name and the reason you won't be in school. It's so easy. And as long as you don't do it every day no one ever checks. Which is good, because if they did they would think I was dying with the number of 'doctor's appointments' I have been to so far this year. Flo's a bit weird about skiving and doesn't like writing in the registration book because she doesn't like people knowing her business. So it went down like a ton of bricks when I once wrote that she was out for an afternoon because she had 'agonising period pains". She went nuts, which is really unlike Flo. She stormed off and everything. I chased after her and made jokes about her being hormonal. It made her even more angry, but she laughed about it eventually. That's usually how it goes with us.

Usually.

I feel bad about the conversation about uni, though. Because, even though I pretended not to notice, I know she was hurt. The thing is, I have been trying to say something for ages, but Flo is so intense about organising our future. She talks about it all the time. I'm finding it really difficult, because it's obvious that we are totally different when it comes to what we want out of life. All I want to do is be excited about not having to do what people tell me to do for once, and all Flo wants is to study more and be told what to do for as long as possible.

It feels like the rest of my life is about to start. In one way it's been getting harder and harder for me to move forward, but in another I know I'm about to break away, so I feel freer than ever. It's exciting, and it's scary too. I know university is the obvious next step but to be honest, if an A level in Classics is too much for me then any degree is sure to make my brain explode. The idea of university sounds like three years more of everything I want to escape. I just don't want to go.

But I do want to leave Guernsey, and I can't wait for that. I just want to know what will become of me, where I will go, who I will meet, what I will do. Life will change so much and that thrills me. I feel like a cannon about to be fired, but until I am lit I have to sit still, and wait. Luckily, inside this barrel I have plenty to do. Guernsey is fun. Since turning eighteen last month I get into pubs. I get off with loads of boys. I have Flo. But the sense that there could always be more is a constant itch.

I sit at a desk at the back of my Classics class and remind myself to make the most of the next few months. I have to fill it with fun. And why not start now, with the thing I enjoy more than anything else: flirting.

As Mr Walker, our midget Classics teacher, turns to write something on the white board, I am sat at a desk on the back row in between Pete Westfield and Marcus Smith. They both fancy me but I wouldn't touch either of them with a barge pole. Marcus has nose hair and Pete is the most blatant virgin I have ever met. I flirt shamelessly with them in this class and then avoid them everywhere else. They don't seem to have a problem with that at all so I don't feel bad. It's all this talk of valiant fighting and goddesses of love that makes us all horny. We also draw lots of diagrams of how we imagine it looks when Mr Walker has sex with a normal-sized person. Needless to say, sex talk is always on the agenda in Classical Civilisation.

'Higher, higher,' urges Marcus as I hitch my skirt up a little bit more.

'Come on, show us your fanny,' whispers Pete, panting.

I lift the hem of my skirt a little higher. We have played this game before, and I am never quite sure if they are joking or not.

'Come on,' presses Pete. 'Just show us your lips.'

OK, too far. Joke over.

'Get lost. I'm not the kind of girl who gets her fanny out just because a boy tells me to, you pair of pervs.'

They try to act cool and pretend they never thought I would actually show them, but I know otherwise. They were both sitting forward to hide their erections and no boy has their tongue out like Pete did unless they think there might actually be a vagina on its way. Men are so simple.

I am realising more and more that all boys think about is fannies and tits. Being a teenage girl comes with serious hurdles, but being a teenage boy involves being obsessed with body parts that are not even part of your own body. What a drag that must be.

Don't get me wrong, I find myself spending at least sixty-five per cent of my time thinking about boys, but I can shut that down if I need to. And I would rather not think about a penis unless it's attached to someone I actually fancy. But for boys, it's all they talk about. At Tudor Falls School for Girls we didn't think about sex that much. Here, there is sex everywhere. The amount of times I've walked into the common room and seen a group of lads huddled in the corner looking at pictures of Pamela Anderson's boobs is unbelievable. You don't see girls looking at pictures of men's willies, do you? Not in public anyway. Weirdly, I think girls are more likely to look at pictures of women's bodies than men's, because we're all so obsessed with what we will look like when we're grown-ups. It's not really a sexual thing, though.

The older I get the more I realise how different men and women are, and how weird it is that we are supposed to find one person of the opposite sex to spend the rest of our lives with. When you break it down, it's kind of ridiculous.

Flo

A-level Religious Studies is so much harder than the GCSE. I get palpitations just before each class because I panic so badly that I haven't taken enough in and that I won't be able to now before the exams. What with French and History, I've had so much coursework to do. I worry all the time. I just worry and worry and worry, because I have to pass. I want to get off this island, go to uni, get a great job and never have to ask my mother for money ever again. Even though we get on a bit better than we used to, she still makes me feel so guilty every time I ask for anything. I miss being able to ask Dad for stuff. I miss Dad. I don't know if I'm having some weird delayed reaction to his death, but the thought of him fills my head every second of every day, and I dream about him too. Strange dreams, like him turning up in a white coat and saying he has to operate on me. Or him coming into my room and chatting about really mundane stuff, like gardening, but the vision is so real that I wake up saying things like, 'Yes, we should probably cut back the hydrangea bush soon.'

I'm sure the dreams are just a phase. I hope so. I guess it's understandable. But now I'm worried that Renée doesn't want to go to the same uni as me. I could do without that on top of the stress of everything else. If I fail these exams I won't be able to leave the island, but if I do leave the island I might lose Renée. Why is nothing ever simple? Why do I always feel like I am about to lose something?

Well, everything apart from my virginity.

Saying that, I am happy, considering what the last couple of years have thrown in my face. There was Sally pretending to be pregnant by Julian and trying to tear me and Renée apart. Then my dad dying suddenly from a heart attack and then Julian having sex with Renée and then revealing to me he is actually only my half-brother and then running off to live in London for no apparent reason without ever taking a minute to ask me if I was OK. Then there was the drama of moving schools last year, and now the daily panic attacks that come with not having to wear a uniform.

I am glad we've moved schools. I miss Tudor Falls some days, but I am much better here, much more myself. Much freer now that I am not being bullied by Sally, and much more loved than ever before, because I have Renée. Our friendship saved my life. Without her I would have stayed sitting where I was the day Dad died and never been able to move, as if my bum had been welded to the chair. Renée is the kind of friend who is so in your face that you can't escape her. It's intense but lovely. I couldn't live without her. I can't imagine having to make friends all over again. Maybe I could just be a recluse instead.

I have to stop worrying. I need something else to focus on, apart from the impending exams. I need a happier distraction, maybe something like playing an instrument. I could take up the clarinet again. Or swimming. The grammar school has a brilliant inside swimming pool. I am sure I heard something about a new life-saving course starting in the next few weeks. That's perfect – I will take up life-saving! I get my notebook out of my bag and write 'LIFE-SAVING' in huge letters across the top of a new page. I will go and check the noticeboard the minute the bell rings.

When the bell does eventually ring I feel excited about the prospect of my new hobby. I stuff my things into my bag and start to hurry towards the pool area. But just as I leave the RS room I nearly trip over as Kerry Hamilton falls to the ground in front of me. The contents of her bag spill everywhere.

'You tripped me up,' she says from the floor.

'I think you just fell,' I say, kneeling down to help her. 'I really don't think I tripped you up.'

'Not you,' says Kerry, gesturing at someone behind me. Three people loom over us. One girl at the front is particularly intimidating. I think her name is Bernadette Rodgers, and the other two are possibly called Samantha and Anthea, or it could be Andrea. I know so few people in my year.

'God didn't help you then, did he, Kerry?' says Bernadette. Her two stooges laugh. 'You can say all the prayers you like, but he won't stop you smashing your face up when you can't even stand up straight, will he?'

A cold feeling goes down my spine. I know this situation only too well. This was my life most days with Sally.

'I didn't fall over, you tripped me up,' says Kerry weakly, wiping a small drop of blood off her lip.

'Tell it to the altar, you Jesus freak,' says Bernadette, turning on her heel. I want to say something to her, but I don't know what it should be. When she has walked far enough away that I know she can't hear us, I turn to Kerry.

'Are you OK?'

'Yeah, I'm used to it. She does it all the time. She's not drawn blood in a while, but this is nothing new.'

'You seem really chilled out about it.' I say, helping her up.

'Bernadette is angry, and that anger is about herself, not me,' says Kerry. 'She is so confused about her own existence that she needs to attack me for mine. I'm just grateful I have my faith and that I don't have to look for other people to blame.' Kerry gets properly to her feet and brushes at her skirt. 'I can take it,' she says. 'But thank you for being nice, Flo.'

I am surprised she knows my name – flattered, if I'm honest. Kerry and I have been in the same Religious Studies class for a year, but we have never actually spoken. It's easy to do that at the grammar. She is a little more vocal than me in class and often puts her hand up and reads sections from the Bible when we are asked to. She is about a size 12, freckly with strawberry-blonde hair, and she wears penny loafers and a cross around her neck. I wouldn't say she was pretty, but she's not unattractive. She doesn't wear any make-up, but why would she? Those freckles are like her own natural make-up. Even though I bet she hates them – people with loads of freckles always hate them.

'Are you sure you're all right?' I ask one more time.

'Yeah, I'm really fine. I'm used to it. Bless you. Thanks again.'

She gives me a really nice hug. A long, lingering kind. The kind of hug that's actually a cuddle, like a parent would give a child to let them know they were proud. It's been a while since I had one of those.

I watch Kerry walk away. I'd lose it if someone pushed me to the ground and drew blood. It's horrible. But she seems impenetrable. With all my social insecurities and paranoia that everyone hates me, I envy her self-assurance.

Making my way down to look at the noticeboard by the swimming pool, I wonder if I need more than a weekly life-saving lesson to toughen me up.

Renée

Every lunchtime I go to the lay-by across the road from school where everyone smokes. There's a mix of people from my year and the Lower Sixth, with the occasional person from the Fifth Year who is willing to risk getting caught having a fag in their uniform to look cool in front of the rest of us. It's way more fun in the lay-by now that I am in the Upper Sixth. It was kind of boring last year feeling like I had to impress the older kids all the time. But when you're in the top year it's like you have instant power. It's not that I really use that power, but I won't deny that I like how people in the years below automatically treat me with a bit of respect.

There is one guy from the Fifth Year who is a bit of a weirdo. His name is Matt Richardson. He just stands there, doing grunty laughs and smoking fag after fag after fag. He's not really friends with anyone, but I think he just wants to hang around with the cool kids. He doesn't offer much to the conversation and his uniform is always a mess. Though who am I to judge? It's a miracle I never got suspended from Tudor Falls with the state of my uniform.

The boys that come to the lay-by are so laddy – they can barely have normal conversations when there are girls around. I find that a lot with boys – they can't be themselves around girls, but together they have completely different relationships. I guess it's the same with girls. I'm not like I am with Flo with anyone else. And that's another thing that makes me wonder why the hell we are supposed to get together with a person of the opposite sex, when men and women clearly have to force themselves to get on. Even Nana and Pop, who were married for sixty years, had to take a deep breath every time they started a conversation. When Pop died last summer, and Aunty Jo told Nana he had gone, Nana did this really long exhalation and then smiled. The next thing she said was, 'After lunch I'll make the horse fire up the escalator.' A totally random statement that means absolutely nothing. There are no escalators on Guernsey, and Nana has only ever been on one once at Gatwick airport.

It is odd how the mind of someone with dementia works. It's so random. Nana's seemed to go full throttle as soon as Pop got diagnosed with cancer last year. Three months later he had gone, and now she is so many million miles away from reality that I think she might oddly be the happiest she has ever been. There is a horrid time with dementia where people who have it still half know what is going on and half don't. So they go in and out of their new madness and get embarrassed and frustrated. I hated that part with Nana. I never knew what to say and I kept having to leave her on her own so I could go and cry. It all happened so fast. If she ever saw me cry she would cry too, and then ask me why we were crying. How could I tell her it was because she was losing her mind and that she would never get it back? But it's different now, because Nana hasn't a clue about reality; she's mad as a box of frogs and says the funniest things, like that thing about the escalator. It's strange, Nana never seemed happy. But then how could you if you were married to someone like Pop? He controlled her completely. Now she smiles all the time. Wherever her mind has taken her, she likes it more than she did when she was here.

It is here in the lay-by that we smoke loads of Marlboro Red and eat crisps and sausage rolls from the canteen. A few people bring their cars round from the car park so we can squeeze in when it's cold, and occasionally the boys play chicken, which terrifies the life out of me. Chicken is when two drivers race towards each other in their cars and at the last minute someone pulls to the side so they don't have a full-on collision. I am sure the boys must be having us on with how dangerous it actually is – surely they have a secret nod that says who will turn and who will keep driving straight? They must do, otherwise they would all be dead by now. I can't even watch – my imagination can't control itself in moments like that.

I find that I am quite brave when it comes to emotional stuff. Well, that's what Aunty Jo tells me anyway. She says I am brave in the way I think about Mum dying, and brave in how I coped with moving schools. But I am not brave when it comes to anything involving physical danger.

I used to be – I used to jump off high walls into the cold sea – but the older I get the more aware I feel of how mortal I am. I can barely ride a bike without being terrified these days, and even when I drive along the really thin lanes in Guernsey I hold my breath every time a car comes in the opposite direction and play out the entire accident in my head. I have had two really close people to me die and I'm only eighteen. It's hardly surprising I've developed such a strong sense that I am not invincible. So I refuse to do things where I might get killed. Emotionally and socially, however, I am just as ridiculous as I always was. I haven't learned much in the way of self-control.

As I squish my foot over my second cigarette, Meg Lloyd, a regular in the lay-by, asks me for one. For fear of looking uncool I light another, even though my lungs retract at the thought of it.

I really like Meg. She seems pretty cool. Because her entire social life is outside of school she doesn't have that same bitchy air about her that so many of the other girls in our year do. She has her own thing going on. She is – I think – always slightly off her head, but she's a straight-A student. I am in awe of her, to be honest. One of those genius types who looks like a bit of a tramp but whose mind is so sharp she knows about everything. She's in my English class and whenever our teacher, Mr Frankel, mentions a book, Meg has always read it. Somehow she manages to read everything and know everything well in advance of us learning it in class. I like her because she seems so independent.

'What are your plans for the summer then?' she asks me, casually.

'Oh, not sure yet. I'll have to get a job, I suppose. Need to save up for uni.' I feel like a geek for saying that, but I feel like I need to conform. 'Are you going to go away?'

'I don't think so. I'll just stick around here, get a job and a place of my own. That's all I'm aiming for,' she says. I feel instantly annoyed with myself for saying what I thought I should say rather than how I really feel. It would have been so much cooler to have said I didn't really want to go to university.

'We'd better get back,' I say, looking at my watch and stubbing out my cigarette.

'Yeah, not me,' says Meg. 'It's only General Studies this afternoon, so I'm going to give it a miss. See you in English tomorrow.'

'See ya,' I say as I watch her walk away, wishing I could follow her and spy on her all afternoon. Meg's got that couldn't-careless attitude I wish I had but I can't carry off because I care too much about what people think. She fascinates me.

Flo

'So, what news from the lay-by of layabouts?' I ask Renée as I pass her a plate of beans on toast piled high with cheese.

Mum's voice comes booming up the stairs.

'Flo! Flo, are you two eating dinner in your bedroom again? If you spill beans on your duvet you can wash it yourself, all right?'

'I wash my duvet myself anyway,' I mutter as I shut my bedroom door and pretend that didn't happen. 'What were we saying?'

'Will she ever give you a break?' Renée asks.

'Probably not. But at least she doesn't expect me to bring up Abi for her any more. She is single at the moment too. It's always easier when she doesn't have a man making her even crazier.'

It's true, my relationship with Mum is better than it ever was, but what I have learned is that people can improve their relationship without actually having to change. She is still as moody as she ever was, I just handle it better. She acknowledges my existence now, and her default setting isn't to put me down, so that makes things easier. But we will never be friends, not like Renée and her Aunty Jo are – but then they don't have years of mutual resentment between them. Mum and I would have to talk for three years straight to iron out the issues in our relationship, so I'll settle for the occasional pleasantry and short but civil conversations about school.

'So come on, what's the gossip?' I ask Renée again. I love hearing about what goes on in the lay-by, because I am way too scared to go there myself. If you don't smoke there is no point, and even if I did smoke I don't think I would hang out there. It's mostly boys or the coolest girls. I went once and all the boys were asking the girls questions about what sex they had the weekend before. I was so terrified they would ask me in front of everyone that I pretended to feel sick and ran back into school.

'Just the usual. Boys cracking jokes and the girls standing around laughing at them,' says Renée, between huge mouthfuls of beans. 'It's weird, isn't it? The idea that this time next year we just won't be going to school any more? It feels like everything is about to change and even if we wanted it to stay the same we couldn't make that happen. That's it – school is done. We will be on our own.'

I know deep down that when it comes to Renée, I should take what she says with a pinch of salt and know that she loves me more than anyone, and that when she says 'on our own' she doesn't mean that our friendship will be over. But I can't. My head doesn't work that way. I go to the worst-case scenario straight away and right now my head is obsessed with the idea that when school is over, Renée and I will move to different places and our friendship will just be a lovely story we tell people about at dinner parties when we are mums. She doesn't seem bothered about it at all.

'I'm thinking about doing a life-saving course,' I say, after a long silence.

Renée seems to find this absolutely hilarious. She almost chokes on her food.

'Oh my God, I think I laughed so hard a baked bean went up my nostril. A life-saving course? *Why?*' she eventually manages to say.

I explain that I need a distraction from the things I find stressful, that I worry too much, that I panic about the exams, but she can't see the logic in taking another thing on to add to my load. Her brain doesn't work that way – she just thinks the fewer things you have going on the better.

'Life-saving lessons are pointless,' says Renée. 'If you ever actually have to save someone's life you won't remember the lessons, you'll just want to grab them round the neck and drag them out of the water. That's all there is to it. It's just another one of your fads, Flo,' she tells me, having dislodged the baked bean. 'Like when you decided to take up tapestry last year. That was so weird. You were all like, "I'm going to make the biggest ever tapestry of Guernsey." Jesus, it was so random.' She is now on her back with her arms crossed over her stomach choking, or maybe she's laughing. Yup, she's laughing.

And though it pisses me off that she finds it all so funny, I must admit it was a bit bizarre. I mean, tapestry? What *was* I thinking?

Renée

'Mark but this flea, and mark in this,
How little that which thou deniest me is;
It sucked me first, and now sucks thee,
And in this flea our two bloods mingled be.
Thou knowest this cannot be said
A sin, nor shame, nor loss of maidenhead;
Yet this enjoys before it woo,
And pamper'd swells with one blood made of two;
And this, alas, is more than we would do.'

As Mr Frankel finishes reading the first verse of John Donne's 'The Flea' to our English class, he puts his book slowly onto his desk and says, 'So, who can tell me what Donne is talking about in this poem?'

There is silence as everyone thinks before Meg pipes up and confidently says, 'Sex, sir. He is trying to persuade whoever he is with to sleep with him.'

'That's right, Meg. Thank you,' confirms Mr Frankel. The rest of us read over the poem and make 'Oh yeah' and 'Of course' type noises. It's always Meg that works stuff out first.

'And what do you all think now you see that?' Mr Frankel asks.

'I think he sounds like a bit of a sleazebag,' offers Maggie Torrode. We all laugh. He really does, when you realise what he is up to.

I love English. We all do. Mr Frankel is cool, I really like him. He's kind of geeky, and wears trousers with large checks on them, quite tight shirts and colourful ties and big thick-rimmed glasses. He is tall and skinny, but sexy, I suppose, in a nerdy kind of way. He is a great teacher because he doesn't act like a teacher, he just acts like a person who knows way more about English literature than us, but rather than be pretentious with that, he genuinely wants us to know as much as he does.

He has character, which is more than can be said about most teachers. I bet Mr Frankel has a fun social life too, and a girlfriend who does something interesting for a job. He's no 'spring chicken', though, as Nana used to say. I think he's probably about forty, but possibly one of those people who looks a lot younger than they are. He's just fun and quirky, which makes a nice change, because a lot of people in their forties in Guernsey seem quite dull.

There's just the eight of us in Mr Frankel's class and there's a real mix of characters. There is Meg, the cool, stoned brainbox who's read every book on the planet. Penny Mayor – she's head girl – Phillipa Jeffries and Paula Young (best friends and quite geeky) and Martha Hemsworth, the one I am most nervous of; in the Lower Sixth I snogged her boyfriend and she has never forgiven me for it. There is also Maggie Torrode, who speaks with a really strong Guernsey accent. The local Guernsey accent sounds like something between cockney and South African and it mainly involves going up in pitch towards the end of every sentence and saying 'Eh?' at the end of everything. Maggie is funny because she has no filter and just says everything she thinks, but I am terrified of her because she is the kind of person who would punch you in the face if she thought you dissed her. She is surprisingly clever, though. And even though she words things a little differently from how Mr Frankel would probably like, she is usually right.

Also in our class is Emma Morden, the anorexic. Emma is so thin and so ill that it's a surprise to me every time she makes it to class. Sometimes she isn't there, and we all know Mr Frankel already knows why because he never questions where she is. No one mentions it, but we all wonder if she has died. In all honesty, she has looked like she is about to die since the beginning of the sixth form, and even before I came to the grammar I used to see her wandering around Guernsey High Street all skinny and unwell. She has been like this for years. She wears really tight dresses that cling to her body, and I always wonder why she does that to herself when she thinks she is so fat. I don't know if I feel sorry for her or not – it's a tricky one – but it's hard to see a skeleton walking around in a mini skirt without feeling concern.

Anorexia feels really personal to me because of my sister, Nell. Before she went to live with our dad in Spain she was hospitalised because of it. The good thing for Nell was that Aunty Jo came home and my family fell back together – just in time probably. God knows what would have happened to Nell if Aunty Jo hadn't stepped in. She would probably have died.

Maybe Emma will die.

Nell is fine now, so I hear. She speaks to Aunty Jo on the phone every couple of weeks, but I avoid the calls. We never really got on, and even though when she left we cried and hugged, it's still difficult. I think if I saw her it would be OK, but talking on the phone to someone who you have only ever argued with is hard. Conversation doesn't exactly flow, so Aunty Jo passes messages between us. I know that one day we will have to face up to talking, but I don't think either of us are up to it yet.

The eighth person in our English class is me. I often wonder how the other seven would describe me if they had to. 'Loud and full of herself' probably, but I'm not really. It's rare that I walk into a room and don't presume that most people in it are better than me in some way. That isn't to say I hate myself, I'm maybe just a little less confident than I let on. But I don't want to be one of those insecure types who seems unsure of herself and nervous. I don't want people to think I am sad.

It's an all-girl class so everyone feels quite relaxed – apart from Emma, who couldn't look relaxed if she tried – and our discussions can be really heated and fun. It reminds me of the best bits of being at Tudor Falls. Apart from the odd exception, girls are definitely better, and funnier, and sometimes cleverer, when boys aren't around. It's annoying but true. I often wonder, when I am in my English class, why men and women have to be together at all. They seem to bring the worst out in each other.

'He's gagging for it,' blurts Maggie.

Mr Frankel chokes a little, but then we all laugh. I laugh mostly because I worry that if I don't Maggie will throw a book at me.

'She should tell him to do one. It's always the men who are begging for sex,' she continues.

'Not always,' says Martha. '*Some* girls can't help themselves and throw themselves at boys.' She shoots me a deathly stare and confirms she is most definitely not over me getting off with her boyfriend in the Lower Sixth. I pretend I didn't hear her and suck my pen.

'What do you think, Mr Frankel?' I ask. 'Is sex always led by men?'

'Stereotypically, maybe. But as always this is down to what an individual wants, and what they are willing to be convinced of by someone else. Do you think it sounds like he is going to get what he wants in the poem?'

'I think the fact he had to write a poem about it probably means he should just stop,' says Maggie. 'But it's really difficult to stop a guy with a raging hard-on!'

There is a group gasp and Mr Frankel realises he probably should have made this a more formal discussion from the start. But then he cracks a little smile and moves the discussion gently on.

'OK, ladies, now to *Oranges Are Not the Only Fruit*,' he says. 'I would hope you have all read it by now. Who would like to read some out loud for us?'

A sea of hands shoot up into the air, including my own, but

I can't stop thinking about what Maggie said. It really is hard to stop a guy with a raging hard-on, this much I know.

Flo

As usual on Friday afternoon Renée and I hurry into town after school to get chips from Christies. It still feels very grown-up. We used to go to a chippy and eat our chips in fields – now we sit in window seats in posh brasseries and eat our chips off a plate with a swanky brand of mayonnaise that is a little bit more yellow than the one we have at home.

We get bowls of chips and hot chocolates with mini marshmallows on top and I smile at Renée as she shoves about fifteen chips into her mouth at once, then blows through them to try to cool them down.

'What? They're hot,' she says, realising she is being watched. I take one and fuff it before dunking it in the mayonnaise and eating it.

'We've come a long way, you and me,' I say, instantly regretting it.

'All right, Grandma, why are you talking like we are in the war?'

'I just mean we've been through a lot, haven't we?'

She eats another chip. Processes what I have said, and then smiles back. 'We really have. I still can't believe we went to school together for ten years before we became friends. If we had only just said hi to each other once or twice then maybe we could have become friends earlier and not been so unhappy for so long. I just find it so weird that two people who are obviously meant to . . . Flo?'

I have frozen.

'Flo, what is it?'

Unable to speak or move my eyes from where they are fixed, I guide her head around. As it turns I can feel her beaming smile.

'Sally de Putron,' she confirms. 'Look at the state of her.'

'Shit shit shit!' I say as I launch my chair back and swoop my head underneath the table.

'Flo, no! Not after all this time. Get out from under there. She has no hold on you any more. Sit up, let's just wave.'

She is right. Of course she is right. I suffered years of bullying by her until I eventually found the courage to tell her to get lost on the day we got our GCSE results. I am so above her now, so beyond the weak moron who used to let her control me the way that she did. And here I am, sitting eating posh chips with my best friend, and there she is, pushing her kid in her pram. I sit up properly on my chair. I will not hide. No matter how much I want to.

'Look at her. She looks like shit,' grins Renée. 'She's put on so much weight, and where are the fancy clothes? That tracksuit looks like it hasn't been washed in a month. She looks like shit.'

Sally does look exhausted, and a bit fat. She has no make-up on and her clothes are frumpy compared to the trendy ensembles she used to wear. I can't deny it's a bit satisfying to see her look so bad. I feel a smile start to appear across my face, which turns into a stifled laugh as the child in the pram, a year or so old and at a guess a boy, starts screaming and writhing uncontrollably. We can hear it cry through the glass

31

that separates us. An ugly baby, the kind of baby you see in a cartoon who has a massive red face and looks evil. It absolutely looks like the kind of baby I would expect someone like Sally to have. Miserable, needy, mean.

'What a horrible baby,' says Renée, echoing my thoughts.

Sally stops her pram right outside the window where we are sitting and huffs and puffs as she unhooks the straps holding down her very unhappy child. She leans into the pram, gets her ugly baby out and starts to bob it up and down. She is close enough that I can see her skin. It's pock-marked and broken. Renée is right – she does look like shit.

Renée is laughing. She is loving every second of Sally's struggle and 'lack of freedom'. I have to admit, I feel much the same. Seeing her looking so hideous is vindication for all the bitchy things she did to me. I don't even feel sorry for the baby. I just presume they are two miserable people who deserve each other.

But then something changes.

Sally looks up and sees us. I feel my stomach plummet a hundred feet and turn to stone, but Renée raises her hand and waves sarcastically, elbowing me to do the same. I summon the courage, but just as I do Sally turns from us to concentrate on her crying child. It's as if she hasn't seen us at all. She's too busy kissing her baby's face and stroking his hair. She bobs him up and down and says 'shhhh, shhh' into his ear. And soon his grimace turns into a smile and he looks at her and he smiles back at her and he isn't so ugly any more. She kisses him again on the nose, and when she is sure he is calm she stuffs him back into his pram and walks away without even looking at us.

'That was amazing,' says Renée. 'That totally made my day. Imagine having a kid. She has no life. Ha, amazing.' She eats a celebratory chip.

But that isn't what I saw. I saw the worst person in the world being loved and unconditionally relied on. Sally will never be alone. It's made me realise how disposable I feel. Like everything I have could disappear at any minute, and that it probably will when school is finished. I feel even more insecure. I wish I had never seen that.

'Let's get the bill,' I say to Renée. 'I want to go home and watch *Neighbours*.'

'Really? I want to get drunk and celebrate. That was one of the most beautiful things I have ever seen in my life.'

'I want to go home,' I say again. 'And I have to babysit tonight.'

Renée and I walk down the high street together and say goodbye outside Town Church. 'I'm going to run before the time on my car runs out,' she says. I hug her, we say 'I love you' and she goes. I watch her walk away, wishing she could see what I saw. I stand for a few moments until I realise how close the weather suddenly seems, and just like that it starts to rain so heavily that I am soaked through in seconds. I run into a phone box, but to my horror there is someone else already in it that I hadn't managed to see. After some embarrassing screaming and apologising I run across Town Square and into the dry calm of the church. This is better. It's lovely in here.

Like, really lovely.

I tiptoe to the back of the church and take a look around.

There are a few people there, and it's quiet, but not totally silent. There are happy whispers as people laugh about getting out of the rain, but even with that it feels so peaceful. Like I walked through the wardrobe into Narnia. Like another world.

I am not sure I have ever been into a church for no reason. I have been to weddings, Abi's christening, school services and Dad's funeral, so I've never really liked church – it's either boring or sad. But this doesn't feel boring or sad, this feels nice.

I sit on a pew.

At the opposite end there is a woman kneeling on one of the little tapestry cushions. Her head is down, and she has a small smile on her face. I wonder what she is praying for, who she is talking to when her lips move. How nice, I think, to be able to connect so comfortably with someone even though they are not there. I have prayed so many mornings of my life and felt nothing, but who does in a school gym surrounded by classmates and teachers repeating the same words every time? It's so formulaic it's easy to forget that it's supposed to feel spiritual. In RS classes we read about how people pray all the time. People talk to God, they just chat away and ask for answers and signs to help them through life. So she must be doing that, she must be chatting to God.

I slip down onto the cushion in front of me and drop my head. I look around to make sure no one is watching but realise that for once I don't really care if they are. I close my eyes and without even trying to create it, the clearest image of Dad comes into my head, as clear as the dreams, but I know I am awake. He is standing in front of me in his favourite navy suit that he used to wear to work. He looks so happy. Happier

34

than he has looked in any of my dreams. In my dreams there is always a sadness or a simplicity that makes him completely devoid of any of the personality that I used to love about him. But here, as clear as anything, I see my dad at the best he ever was. I look at him and smile, he smiles back and walks away, and then the impetus to start speaking takes over me, and I start to pray.

It could be no less than forty-five minutes later that I open my eyes and stand up. I feel like I have taken a nap, but the reality is that I couldn't have been more awake the whole time. I told him everything, God, I went through it all. And it felt good.

Looking at my watch I see it's seven thirty. I must go home quickly as Mum is going out at eight o'clock and I'm babysitting Abi tonight. The church is completely empty. A part of me doesn't want to leave.

As I make my way to the door I see a noticeboard.

Sunday-morning service at 10 a.m.: all welcome is written on a laminated, yellow page of A4. I make a mental note.

Outside the air is cold but the rain has gone. I walk home feeling different – relieved is a good way to put it. I don't know how it came to be, but I think I just found God.

Or maybe he found me.

Renée

I wake up at twelve thirty. Even though I am used to this now I still have a little moment of appreciation for Aunty Jo, who rarely makes me get out of bed at the weekends. Unlike Pop, who used to make us get up by 9 a.m. for absolutely no reason other than for him, Nana, Nell and I to be all awkward together downstairs.

As my eyes come into focus I look around my bedroom. I love it so much. I have a double bed with big windows, the walls are painted stone and my wardrobe is French-looking – apparently – and painted white. My curtains are from Laura Ashley and my bed linen is a really nice peach colour with little flowers on it. I have a cute dressing table with a nice big mirror and my own make-up drawer that is full of Aunty Jo's cast-offs. I have a hi-fi on the floor and piles and piles of tapes and records and my massive Spice Girls poster on the wall. I even have my own bathroom, which I have never had a single shower in without being grateful for not having to share it with three other people who together smell of sick, BO and old age.

The house is small but perfect. There are three bedrooms, one on the ground floor that Nana sleeps in, one upstairs towards the back where Aunty Jo sleeps, and one to the front, which is mine. Set in the depths of St Martins, the parish that makes the bottom-right foot of Guernsey, it's quiet, very green and feels like the countryside. Our garden is big and we have geese, which I wasn't sure about at first, but they are actually really good guard dogs. If anyone steps into the garden they go ballistic, and I like that. Aunty Jo says she wants to get more animals. 'I like looking after things,' she tells me all the time. And every time she says it I hug her and say thank you. Thank you for looking after me and Nana, and for making our lives the best they have ever been. I owe her everything and I love her so, so much.

But that doesn't mean I don't still miss Mum.

I have these really weird moments where I remember that I can be sad at any given moment. Like today, I go to get out of bed and I see my toes. I painted my nails red last week and when I see them I get butterflies in the back of my nose, like I could cry, just like that. Red nails remind me of Mum. I like having them because when people tell me I remind them of her it makes me happier than anything else, so sometimes I dress a bit like her, or paint my nails, or wear Chanel No. 5. It makes me feel like her. Which is a nice thing, but when I forget I have done it, it can take me by surprise, and that's when I think I might cry out of nowhere.

I talk to her too. I don't know why, really – I know she isn't anywhere, but it just feels good to say hi to her sometimes. So I wish her well every morning and say goodnight before I go to sleep, and sometimes when something is bothering me I tell her about it. It makes me feel better. And Aunty Jo is so like her it's impossible not to think of her every day. Sometimes I hear her laugh in another room and it could be Mum laughing. That's another one of those times when I could cry if I let myself. The feeling crawls through me like bugs under my skin. I have to stop and really focus for the few seconds it takes to pass through my body, and then I am normal again. And that's what I've realised my feelings about Mum are – full body sensations that I can't control but have to live with. It will probably be like this forever now, and I can cope with that. It's much better than the anger Pop was stuck with. That drove him mental half the time.

I put a big jumper on over my PJs and slip my feet into my

slippers. I can hear Aunty Jo downstairs in the kitchen talking to Nana.

'Would you like soup for your lunch, Mum?' she asks as I get to the kitchen door.

'All the way to the left,' answers Nana. Aunty Jo smiles and pours a tin of Heinz tomato soup into a saucepan.

'Morning everyone,' I say, entering the room and kissing Nana on the head. 'I slept late.'

'You did. Do it while you can. Bacon?' asks Aunty Jo.

'I partied with the best of them all night long,' Nana tells me. 'I could have thrown the lot of them in the water.'

'I'm sure you could, Mum. Renée, I am going to a car boot sale tomorrow morning down at L'Ancresse. Do you want to come and help me? You could sell all your old clothes and make some money,' says Aunty Jo, stirring the soup and adding a splash of cream to it.

'That would be amazing. Can Flo come? She has so many clothes I really want her to get rid of.' I laugh. Flo's clothes are so funny. She buys one top and wears it every time we go out for six months, then buys another one and does the same. And the kinds of things she buys for school are boring. She gets things that look as close to school uniform as possible because she finds having to wear our own clothes every day so hard.

'Of course,' says Aunty Jo. 'Let's just fill the car up and make some cash.' She walks a bowl of soup over to the table, takes the fork that Nana intends to eat it with out of her hand and replaces it with a spoon.

I take the cup of tea and bacon sandwich Aunty Jo has made me and go into the hall to the phone. Still yawning a bit, I look up Smellies in the phone book. It's the shop where Flo works on Saturdays. All they sell is candles, joss sticks, incense burners and essential oils. Flo always smells like she's been dunked in perfume on Saturday nights. I dial the number. Mora, her moody boss, answers.

'Hello, is Flo there, please?' I ask Mora.

'Renée, how many times have I asked you not to call Flo when she is working? Saturday is our busiest day. It had better be important!'

'It's really important,' I tell her. 'I am calling on behalf of her mum who can't get to the phone because of her broken hip.'

I hear the phone get put down and then the sound of rustling as Flo picks it up.

'Hello?' she whispers, even though the boss knows she is on the phone. 'Renée, what's happened? Is it Abi?'

'Nothing is wrong with Abi, you moron. You know I always have to make up a reason for calling you at work or Mora just hangs up on me.'

'Oh, right. Well, why are you calling me at work?'

'Aunty Jo is doing a car boot sale tomorrow morning. She said we can take some of our clothes to sell and make some money. Fancy flogging those burgundy DM boots of yours? I think it's time.'

'I can't.' She pauses. 'I'm going to church.'

'You're what?' I ask, through a mouth full of bacon and bread.

'I am going to go to church tomorrow. It's Sunday. That's church day,' she says, as if this is normal.

'Wait, when did you start going to church?'

'I don't know. I mean, I haven't started yet. Renée, I am just going to church, OK?' She is still whispering, even though she is getting all het up.

'Um, OK. Well, do you want to come and see me at work tonight? We can get into The Monkey free and I'll sneak you drinks?'

'OK, but I can't get too drunk. I don't want to be hungover tomorrow. I have to go. Don't call me at work again. Mo—' I hear Mora telling her to finish. 'I love you,' she manages to sneak in before the line goes dead.

I sit on the stairs staring at the front door, trying to process that conversation. Church? Is there a christening I don't know about?

'Renée, feed this to the geese, will you?' says Aunty Jo, shoving a bucket full of soggy bread under my nose. 'You can take Nana. Just watch she doesn't try to sit on Freddie again.'

As I guide Nana down the garden path, still wearing my pyjamas but with the addition of wellies and a coat, she tells me all about the time she saw a penguin chase an airplane along the high street by St Michael's. She really is very sweet with her funny little stories. I'm sure there is truth in there somewhere. It was probably a nun riding a bike or something. Or maybe she did see a penguin chase an airplane along the high street by St Michael's. None of us will ever know now. I nod and smile and sound fascinated and amazed. It's the least I can do.

'Here you go, Nana. Here are the geese. We are going to give them their lunch now.'

I leave her holding onto the fence and I open the gate, walking into the area where the geese live. Nana waits patiently to see what I am going to do next, totally forgetting what we are at the end of the garden for. I turn the bucket upside down and all the soggy bread flops out and covers my wellies in slop. 'Look, Nana,' I call. 'I got it all over my wellies.' She laughs excitedly but soon forgets why. I carry the empty bucket back over to her, shut the gate behind me and we watch as Freddie and Clara eat their food.

'They mate for life you know, Nana. Aunty Jo told me. Geese fall in love, like humans do. They find the One and stay with them forever. Isn't that sweet?'

She stares at them. Their long, lean necks bending down, their beaks chomping on their meal of tasteless nothingness that they don't seem to mind. And then Nana, like her mind is clear as a bell, says, 'That doesn't mean they found the right goose.'

2

Who Do You Think You Are

Renée

I have worked in The Ship and Crown – or The Ship as it is more commonly known – pub for a couple of months now. My shift starts at 7 p.m. and what to wear is always an issue. I get the dregs of pints sloshed all over me as I put the glasses in the dishwasher, and by about 10 p.m. everyone is so hammered that I get all sorts spilt on me as I have to make my way through them all to get to the tables, so black usually hides that the best. I never wear short skirts – not any more – not just because drunk men can't help themselves and someone always puts their hand up it, but also because I had a terrible incident with a piece of toilet paper one night. I unexpectedly got my period so went to the loo and folded some loo roll up to put in my knickers. There I was just happily serving pints when I realised it had fallen out. There was basically a bright-red papier mâché of my labia on the floor behind the bar. I couldn't pick it up because if I bent down everyone would have seen my bloody knickers. So I kicked it under the fridge, and I very much suspect that it's still there. Since then, no skirts at work. It's just too complicated. I also have a few body issues I need to factor into my outfit choices at the moment. My legs are as skinny as ever, but my belly is getting flabbier.

I find the more layers I wear the less self-conscious I feel. When you spend Saturday nights weaving in and amongst drunk men in a pub you get touched around your waist a lot. I don't like it. Although it's gentle, there is always something presumptuous in the way they do it. It isn't really about helping me get past or asking me to get out of their way – it's about sex. I find that if you make eye contact with a man, and hold it just that little bit too long, then he will think you fancy him and suddenly he is everywhere you go. The drunker he gets, the more he looks, the more he presumes your accidental eye contact was intentional. You have to really watch yourself around drunk men when you work in a pub – they are fun and everything, but it's annoying when they get the wrong idea. They don't leave you alone all night after that. When I am drunk too I don't mind so much, but when I am sober and working it's just a pain in the arse.

By nine thirty the pub is completely full and Flo is sitting at the end of the bar in her usual spot, wedged into a corner and on her own. Most people know she is a friend of mine so it isn't too lonely for her. Also, she turned eighteen in December so there is no issue with her looking suspicious. Sometimes she gets chatting to other punters, but mostly she sits there drinking the drinks I sneak her and waits for me to finish so we can go to The Monkey. Sneaking her drinks is easy. I pour an extra shot of vodka every time I serve someone a big round. I leave it next to the soft-drink gun, then Flo orders a Coke from me, I pour it into the glass with vodka in it and just charge her for the Coke. It's flawless. The only problem is that Flo can't take her drink, so if she has too much she often falls off her chair. One time I even had to carry her out at the end of the night. I told my boss, Dave, I thought her drink had been spiked, she was that bad. So now I pace what I give Flo, and sometimes if I think she has had too much, I give her a shot of water instead of vodka and she never knows the difference. I, on the other hand, can handle my drink. So I keep a bottle of vodka in the cellar for when I have to change barrels and get new bottles of spirits. Needless to say, by the time my shift is over at midnight Flo and I are usually pretty wasted. And that is great, because the major perk of working in a pub is that you get on the guest list of The Monkey nightclub.

'We've been working tonight,' I say to Max the big, scary bouncer. Who I snogged last New Year's Eve but who refuses to acknowledge it now.

'Your mate is too drunk,' he says, looking at Flo, who isn't doing too badly, but one eye is definitely starting to droop.

'She's fine. It was just a busy night in the pub. We're tired, right, Flo?' I subtly elbow her in the ribs and she perks up.

'No, I'm not drunk. Just overworked and underpaid,' she says in a weird cockney accent that comes out of nowhere.

'I'm getting you a Red Bull,' I tell her, as we go down the stairs and into the club.

The Monkey is cool and we come here most Saturday nights after I finish work. The DJ plays the same music every night and the same people are always there. I guess that is to be expected on a small island, but a new face stands out a mile and sexy people get pounced on so it's a bit of a meat market sometimes, and there aren't many rules as to how far people can go. The club is divided in half by a dance floor with a narrow walkway down one side and a sofa along the wall. A few weeks ago a couple were going for it in front of everyone on the dance floor and people were walking past the whole time. The guy had his hand down the girl's pants. A few people took photos and Flo and I were staring in disbelief. I'm all for snogging in public, but they were practically shagging. We even saw the top of her pubes, but she was so drunk she didn't seem to care. When the guy decided he was finished and stood up, she rolled off the sofa onto the floor and lay there for about three minutes before finding the strength to get herself up, by which time the audience had dispersed and everyone was back to dancing. Flo and I went over to see if she needed a hand, but all she said was, 'Why would I need your help?' To which I said, 'Um, I dunno. Because you just got fingered in a nightclub and the guy who did it is now over there grinding someone else?' But she seemed nonplussed and stumbled to the toilets, where I presume she threw up. But that's The Monkey for you. A meat market that is open until 2 a.m., plays cheesy pop music and turns a blind eye to public displays of foreplay. I love it.

As we get to the bar the Spice Girls' 'Who Do You Think You Are' comes on and Flo and I give up on getting a drink and run to the dance floor. We love the Spice Girls so much, and every time we hear one of their songs we have a rule to stop whatever it is we are doing and dance. 'You're the shy one!' I shout in Flo's ear. 'Shy Spice!' She shrugs her shoulders as if accepting it.

'You're the naughty one!' she shouts back. 'Bloody Naughty Spice!'

We let rip on the dance floor. Jumping around like our lives depend on it. I love it when Flo gets like this – she abandons all inhibition and just goes for it. It's the mix of booze, the Spice Girls and the fact that it's quite dark in The Monkey. I watch her, aware not to make her feel self-conscious. She is so beautiful, a surprisingly funky dancer and sexy too. Her body is gorgeous, but you would never notice it under the clothes she wears. She is much thinner than me, with big boobs, long legs, gorgeous long brown hair. The only problem with Flo is that she doesn't see herself the way she should. She is racked with insecurity, and it holds her back every day. But in other ways she is the strongest person I know, the most grounded. She would be the best person in the world if she just had a bit of faith in herself.

I jump closer to her and lean forward, and she leans back and we start a rock-and-roll-type move, singing along. We know all the words. I throw my hands in the air one more time and, as the disco lights shine directly into my face, I spot him. Dean Mathews. About twenty-five. Tall, handsome and intriguing. He is a writer for the *Guernsey Globe* – he wears blazers and neck scarves. He has floppy curly hair and when I think about having babies when I am older, I think of him being the dad.

He comes into the pub and I see him around all the time. But we have never actually spoken.

I stare at him, trying to get him to make eye contact. Flo is now going crazy to 'Let Me Be Your Fantasy', and I am in a bubble. I keep looking at Dean. Right now, having a man think I want him by catching his eye is fine by me. I want him to know I want him, and I want him to want me back. I hold my gaze firm on his face. After a few seconds he feels it and looks over. He turns slightly so he is facing me head on and he watches me dance. Wow, that was easy. Now I need to keep his interest. So, like Madonna in the 'Papa Don't Preach' video when she dances around in those black pedal pushers and strapless top, I break into that routine. Flo and I learned it a few months ago and this feels like as good a time as any to do it. He watches me as I prance around doing my best to keep the eye contact going throughout. The routine doesn't quite fit to the music but the song couldn't be more perfect. I want to be his fantasy. I lose myself in it, I let the music take me. He watches me the whole time. I feel so sexy. When the song ends I stop dancing, look to Flo, who is totally lost in the music, and decide to go over to him. How will he ever be the father of my children if I don't go over and say hi? As I push my way through the dancers I stop when out of nowhere Dean turns around and Meg Lloyd swoops in. They hug, then turn to the bar and order a drink.

Shit.

That was not supposed to happen.

'I LOVE THIS ONE!' screams Flo in my ear as she bounces up behind me, unaware of what I have just been through. I

47

stand still, deflated, gutted.

'What's wrong?' Flo asks me, slowing down a little. 'What's the matter?'

I take a few seconds to collect myself.

'We need to learn some new dance routines,' I say. 'Let's get that drink.'

Flo

I wake up fully clothed on top of the covers and my brain feels like it's about to explode. I bash my hand around looking for my glass of water, but instead of the hard, flat surface of my bedside table my fingers fall into a wet, squishy orifice.

'Get the hell out of my mouth!' yells Renée as she thumps me on the chest.

'Sorry! I thought you were a table. I forgot I was here. Please, get me water.'

Renée rolls over onto her side and falls to the floor, landing on all fours. I can't move to watch, but I hear her crawl over to her dressing table, pick up a glass and crawl back with it.

'Thanks. I can't believe you managed that.'

'I barely remember doing it,' she says as she buries her head into her pillow and makes whimpering noises.

'I am going to die,' I tell her.

'I think I'm already dead,' she replies.

We lie still for another three minutes until Renée falls out of bed again. This time I make out the word 'bacon' as she heads for the door.

I lie on her bed trying to focus on the ceiling. As I start to make out the details of the light I feel that I might actually survive the day.

'Can I borrow some clothes?' I shout after her. She mumbles a yes.

Somehow I manage to get to the wardrobe. As I catch a glimpse of myself in the mirror I wonder if going to church for the first time looking like a stop-out with a hangover is such a good idea. I riffle through Renée's wardrobe and find a black knee-length skirt and a black shirt. I have never seen her wear either of them. I wore black boots last night so all in all, the outfit works fine. I go into the bathroom where I have a wee, tie back my hair, splash my face with cold water and clean my teeth with Renée's toothbrush. I am going to be OK. I can do this, I think. I follow the smell of bacon downstairs.

'Why have you dressed like you're going to a funeral?' says Renée from the floor, where she is lying. Her aunty Jo smiles at me as she offers me a bacon sandwich. I take it.

'I need to look smart. I'm going to church,' I say, expecting to be laughed at. Instead Renée drops her head back to the floor.

'Well, don't forget to thank God for bacon,' she says, her mouth full.

'You could come with me?'

'The place would blow up if I walked in the door. It's a certain kind of life you live when you never have to worry about what your mother would say,' Renée says, giving me a painful-looking wink.

'Well, your aunty says you should pull yourself together and go and get ready for the car boot sale. Come on, up,' says

Jo, physically trying to get Renée upright.

'Bye then,' I say as I leave. 'Thanks for the bacon, Jo.'

'Tell him I'll see him soon,' shouts Renée's nana after me.

Who?

After having to get off the bus at Trinity Square so that I could puke in a bin, the ten-minute walk to Town Square does me good, and by the time I get there I feel a lot better. There are quite a few people standing outside, all dressed in their Sunday best. The church looks very different to how it usually does on the days when the shops are open. Usually it's Guernsey's dodgiest inhabitants hanging around there; today it looks like Guernsey's finest. I excuse myself as I walk through them all, head into the church, take a *Book of Common Prayer* from a lady who is handing them out, and take a seat on a pew reasonably near to the back. I am aware that my breath smells of booze.

No one is talking now, apart from some children. But even they seem to know to keep the volume down as people all around us are on their knees telling God whatever it is that is on their mind.

There is a clarity here that comes from being surrounded by people you know believe in the afterlife. I don't feel silly for believing that Dad is out there somewhere when I am in here. But thinking of him in heaven doesn't make me any less aware of the fact that he isn't on earth. When people die they disappear from your life, we all know that. And that is what families are for, they're the ones who gather round you and help you not forget that person. They're the ones who help you keep their memory alive. But not my family. Mum almost refuses to mention him, and Abi was only four when he died, so she only remembers him a little. I try to tell her about him, and teach her about who he was, but he's just a distant memory now. Mum hasn't helped me with that.

Sometimes I wonder if me trying to make Abi remember him is cruel. Why do I try so hard to give her a person to miss, to be sad about? Maybe it's a good thing that over time she won't remember him at all. How can you spend a lifetime being sad about someone you barely knew?

The things I remember make it impossible to forget him. I remember how his cuddles felt, I remember the feeling of his lips on my cheek when he kissed it. I remember the details of his voice so acutely that when I go to bed at night I can make him whisper in my ear. I remember the taste of his dinners, his terrible jokes, the way he danced to ABBA. I remember him telling me I was his favourite person in the world, and that he would always have my back. And I knew that no matter what happened in the rest of my life, I would never need more than that love from my dad. And when he died it vanished, and so did my safety net. And ever since, even though I have Renée, I have felt a bit lost. And I don't feel like I am allowed to feel like that any more, not still, not nearly three years later. So I hide it all and I say I'm fine, and I look for things to take my mind off him, like tapestry or life-saving. And I just try really, really hard to keep his memory alive in my head. The only place he still exists. Apart from here, maybe.

Can he see me?

I smile, just in case.

Then someone taps me on the shoulder and I jump so badly I

nearly have a heart attack myself. It's Kerry from school, sitting in the pew behind me. Her freckles look particularly brown and she is wearing a pale blue, long-sleeved dress.

'Hey,' she says cheekily. 'Come to church to find me, did you?'

'No,' I say abruptly. 'I am here for the service.'

She shuffles round and sits next to me on my pew. I don't want her to. I was looking forward to doing this on my own, having the space to work out if this is for me or not. I enjoy the way I can think here, I don't want someone chatting over my thoughts or pushing me into anything too religious. I suddenly feel like I shouldn't be here. Dad, I think. Make her leave me alone.

She doesn't go away.

'Thanks so much for helping me at school the other day,' she says. She seems a lot more confident here than she did there.

'I didn't do anything. I thought you might have hurt yourself when you fell, that's all.'

'Well, thanks anyway. And thanks for not kicking me while I was down. I am used to it, but very few people at school have much sympathy for us "Jesus freaks". Is your church closed?' she asks.

'Closed?'

'Is that why you are here? Because your church is having refurbishments?'

'No. I don't have a church. It's my first time.'

'Wow, you're a virgin?'

I feel myself flush. It's a new thing that my face has started doing since I got to the grammar. If anyone says the slightest thing that embarrasses me, or sometimes even if a teacher just speaks to me in front of the class, my face explodes with red. I feel the blotches start in hot patches on my neck and then immediately creep up my face. The heat is instant, like someone has tipped my head to the side, poured boiling water into my ear and put a plug in like a hot-water bottle. I can do nothing to stop it, I just have to breathe steadily to try to control my thumping heart and not touch my face. And here I am now, in church, fluorescent and drenched in sweat in seconds because someone just asked me *that* question. I make a weird croaky sound instead of words.

'Oh, no,' Kerry says, looking quite embarrassed herself. 'No, I didn't mean that. I mean a church virgin. It's what my friends and I call people who come for the first time.'

The plug is gently removed from my ear, and the water pours out. We share an awkward laugh.

'I have a bit of a complex about that, obviously,' I say, blowing on my palms to dry them.

'Well, you're in good company here. There are loads of virgins at church.'

The organ starts playing and a vicar walks down the aisle.

'Chat after?' says Kerry, hopping back to the pew behind me.

'Sure.'

After we sing 'All Things Bright and Beautiful' – I feel proud that I know the words – the vicar does a sermon about how people will love you, and you will love them, but you can never rely fully on another person because their own life will always be their priority. He then tells us that we are all God's priority, and that we can rely on him completely. God will never have something more important to do than take care of us. He tells us that if we commit fully to God, he will commit fully to us. 'Have realistic expectations of those with whom you surround yourself,' he says. 'But know that God is the only one you can ever really rely on.'

I was expecting to find the sermon boring, but it isn't. What he says is what I need to hear – it helps me understand the meaning of what God could do for me. It gives me the feeling that I could actually connect with Him, and not just the idea of Him.

At the end, as Kerry and I step outside, the day seems brighter, crisper. Maybe it's just the impact of being inside for over an hour, but I feel spritely, energised. Really glad I came to church.

'It doesn't have to just be Sundays,' says Kerry, pulling on her coat. 'If you think this is for you, there's a small group of us who meet on Thursday nights at one of our houses. We pray together, read from the Bible. You are welcome to join if you want to.'

'Maybe,' I say doubtfully. Praying in a group? I mean, I know that's essentially what church is, but in someone's living room? That sounds odd.

'It's a bit like a book club I guess, but we only study one book.' She laughs. 'What the vicar said was true – God is the only one who will never let you down. Hopefully our group will make you feel the same way about us, though. We're friends and we share our experience of God. It's nice. It would be nice to get to know you better too. Oh look, there are the guys.'

She waves frantically at three other people, two boys and a girl. The two boys couldn't look more different. One is tall and skinny and looks about twenty-four, the other is short and stocky and I think I recognise him from school. The girl is plump and looks like she is probably part of a drama club; they always wear black T-shirts, DM boots and look like they never brush their hair.

'Guys, this is Flo. It's her first time today and I just invited her to Bible group on Thursday,' Kerry says. 'Flo, this is Sandra, Matt . . . and Gordon.' They all nod enthusiastically and the older one, Gordon, reaches out to shake my hand. He is tall and skinny, with a rock-and-roll T-shirt on.

'Looking forward to having you in the Bible group, Flo,' he says. 'It will be good for us to have a new energy in the group.'

'Well, if it's energy thatcha need, it's what I got,' I say to the *Record Breakers* theme tune. I am trying to sound confident and upbeat, but I immediately hate myself for sounding like such a prat. What's worse is that nobody even laughs, which obviously makes me feel even more of a prat. Renée would be on the floor after that.

I think about what Kerry said. A group of friends to share this with might be really nice. Maybe I don't have to do this on my own. Like the vicar said, I need to fully embrace God for him to fully embrace me, and these guys have obviously nailed it. They could teach me how. God might be the only person I can rely on when school finishes, the only thing I can take with me wherever I go.

'All right,' I tell them. 'I'd love to come. Thanks.'

'Great, see you Thursday then,' says Kerry, writing down an address in a notebook and ripping it out for me. 'Seven until 9 p.m. So happy you're coming!'

'Come on, Nana. Let's go and get a burger,' I say, rolling out of the back of Aunty Jo's car when we arrive at L'Ancresse, where about twenty-five other cars are lined up with their boots open.

'It's ten o'clock in the morning. You had your second bacon sandwich half an hour ago. Are you serious?' questions Aunty Jo.

I am deadly serious. I don't know what it is about hangovers that means my stomach loses the capacity to feel full, but I need to keep consuming or I might collapse. I lead Nana by the elbow and steer her to the burger van. She stands and watches me eat my body weight in beef, ketchup and bread, all the while telling me that it is important for me to breathe into my food.

By the time we get back to Aunty Jo she has organised all of our bits and bobs in the boot of the car, put a little deck chair out for Nana and is pouring cups of tea from a flask for us all.

'Sit here until you get too cold, Mum,' she says. 'Then you can sit in the car with the heating on.' She turns to me and says, 'She could sit out all night in that fur coat of hers. It's either warm blood or the fact she can't remember from second to second that she is freezing. In case it's the latter, keep your eye on her. If her lips go blue we will get her in.' Aunty Jo stuffs a blanket around Nana's legs and carries on arranging things. It's surprisingly chilly for April.

There is everything. Old clothes, books, kitchen things. 'A lot of this was left in the house before we moved in,' Aunty Jo tells me, passing me a kettle that's so black on the bottom

I wonder why anyone would buy it. She whacks a sticker on it that says £1 and tells me to put it to the front.

'What's this?' I ask, pulling a picture frame out of a bag. There is a picture of her and Uncle Andrew in it.

'Oh, that. Take the picture out and put it in the bin. We could get a tenner for that frame, it's solid silver.'

I do as she says, but carefully. As the photo comes out a key falls to the ground. On the back of the photo is some writing. *Two Peas in a Pod, The Crane 1984 – our honeymoon. Room 341.*

'What does the "Two Peas" mean?' I ask her, mesmerised by how happy they look in the photo.

'It's what I used to call us, because I thought we were so similar. Like two peas in a pod. But it was all wrong.'

'What do you mean? How could being the same be all wrong?'

'Because we weren't similar at all, we were completely different,' says Aunty Jo. 'But I changed myself to try to be like him so he would love me. I never trusted that he loved me so I tried to be someone I wasn't, someone like him. That didn't excite him, so hate became the only way to get passion into the marriage.' She pulls a cable from a bag and seems upset when there is nothing attached to the end of it. 'So he started to hate me.'

I can't imagine anyone hating Aunty Jo. She is the best person in the world.

'Do you believe that everyone has one person they are supposed to be with for life?' I ask her. 'It feels like such an impossible thing. Men and women are so different.'

'I think it is good for everyone to have one person they can rely on, no matter what,' says Aunty Jo. 'And being different is no bad thing. Men are hard work, though; if you don't find the right one, you can live a life of misery. You have to find one who accepts you for everything that you are, and not what they would like you to be. And you have to find one who thinks your experience of life is as important as theirs, otherwise you will resent them, and that's the worst way to be. But I would like to meet someone, and get it right next time.' Her eyes well up a little. She shakes her face and snaps herself out of it. 'But I have you and Mum and the geese. What more do I need, really?' she finishes, managing a smile.

'Yes, you have us,' I say, knowing that Nana won't be around forever and that in six months' time I will be off to start the next chapter of my life. For the first time I find myself worrying about her. Who will look after Aunty Jo when we have gone?

I hold the photo in my hand and try to imagine who my 'One' will be. Will I choose him right? And if I don't, will I end up alone, or will I just live with someone forever that I find boring and who doesn't interest me at all? I see both Nana and Aunty Jo and how they married the wrong people. How can you not be angry that you wasted all of that time?

'Well, I'm glad it didn't work out, because if it did then God knows where I would be if you hadn't come home,' I say, putting my arm around her shoulder and kissing her cheek.

'Me too,' she says. 'And it didn't kill me, did it? Coping with a bit of heartache is the least I can do.' She holds a scarf that belonged to Mum. 'I don't know what I should keep and what I should get rid of. It seems so strange that this could be worn by someone else, who has no idea that it was hers.'

'Then let's keep it,' I say. 'Let's keep everything we have left. Pop threw so much away when she died and he shouldn't have. We don't have to look at this every day, but we can keep it. And those dresses in your wardrobe, and her jewellery. Let's pack it away when we get home, but let's not sell anything else.'

Aunty Jo agrees. It is strange that she even brought the scarf today, but I think she thought maybe getting rid of stuff was a good idea. It isn't, though. We have already lost enough.

'I miss her so much, Renée,' she says. 'My darling sister, the poor girl. There was nothing I could do to protect her when she got sick. We looked out for each other all our lives. I felt so useless.'

She is crying now, trying to hide it from Nana who is watching everyone busy around. It's weird for me when Aunty Jo cries about Mum. It reminds me that she wasn't just my mum – she was someone's daughter, someone's sister. It's as hard for Aunty Jo as it is for me. Maybe harder, I don't know. She knew her longer than I did.

'You must call Nell,' she says abruptly. 'I know you girls didn't get on, Renée, but she is your sister. You two don't realise how precious you are to each other. If I had known I would lose Helen I don't think I would ever have left Guernsey. It all just feels like such a waste of time now. I left to be with a man who didn't even want me, and because of that I missed out on the last few years of my sister's life. You and Nell have to make the most of each other, be friends. No one will ever be to you what your sister can be. One day you will realise how much you love her and you'll understand why you have to stick together.'

I hug her. Making promises about my relationship with Nell isn't something I am comfortable with, so I don't say anything. I don't know if Nell and I will ever be what Mum and Aunty Jo were.

She pulls herself together, smiles at Nana and passes me a bag of stickers and tells me to make up prices for everything. I stick £40 on the silver photo frame and turn to see if anyone is looking like they might buy something. A lady carrying a basket full of little brown paper bags walks past shouting, 'Homemade fudge!' I pretend not to notice, but Nana's face lights up like she just won a million pounds.

'You remember what fudge is, don't you, Mum?' says Aunty Jo, laughing and handing me a fiver.

Brilliant, I think. I haven't eaten anything for at least fifteen minutes.

'So the banana bar symbolises a penis and how the two lesbians in the shop and Jeanette will never marry men?' asks Meg.

'Exactly,' says Mr Frankel. 'The author is making subtle references to the phallus here, and setting up for the revelation of Jeanette's sexuality later in the story.'

I watch Meg from across the classroom. All I can think about is her and Dean and how I am determined to find out if he is her boyfriend or not. I've asked almost everyone in our year if she is going out with anybody, but no one knows anything about her. Dean had looked so happy to see her that night at The Monkey. I didn't see them kiss, but they stayed together all night and neither of them spoke to anyone else. They left together about half an hour before the club shut, but I couldn't tell if they were holding hands or not.

It's doing my head in. He was obviously flirting with me that night and he comes into the pub on his own all the time and eyes me up – he can't be in a relationship. I have such a massive crush on him. I need to know if he is single or not. I have to be brave to find out. I tear a piece of paper out of my notebook.

Hey Meg, how are you? Wanna come to the lay-by with me after English? Renée x

I throw it at her and wait for a response. Even by my standards this is very random and she is fully entitled to ignore it, as we go to the lay-by almost every time after English, so this note is creepy and unnecessary. I watch her read it. She looks at me, nods, then starts to write. A minute or so later she chucks the note back. Mr Frankel turns round seconds later, but Meg seems completely unfazed about the idea of getting caught.

Sure. And are you free Saturday night? Dean asked me to invite you to see the play he has written. There's a performance of it at the Youth Theatre at 7.

My eyeballs nearly fall out of my head. He asked her to ask me? Did this really just happen? If that wasn't a lesson in the value of being bold I don't know what is. I could do a star jump here and now. They are just friends. Breathe, Renée. Oh my goodness, he is so obviously going to be the father of my children. I instantly devise an excuse to get out of work on

Saturday night and throw a note back to Meg saying, *Cool, yeah. I'd love to, thanks.*

I open my copy of *Oranges Are Not the Only Fruit* and try to focus on what Mr Frankel is saying.

'A girl is particularly vulnerable when she can't rely on the support of her mother,' he says, posing a question to the class about whether the mother's treatment of Jeanette is cruelty or just tough parenting. But my focus is elsewhere. I spend the rest of the class staring out of the window imagining Dean putting shelves up in the big house we will live in when we get married and have babies.

In the lay-by after class I manage not to fire a load of questions at Meg about Dean. I can wait until Saturday now. I must try to be cool. We stand smoking a fag, listening to Pete and Marcus talking about a girl that Pete claims to have fingered at the weekend whose fanny smelt of blue cheese. It's so obvious he hasn't got a clue what he's talking about.

'It's out of order, you know? The way you talk about girls. It's actually your dicks that smell of cheese, so you can shut up,' I say.

'Oooooo, got your period, have you?' retorts Pete. That classic immature response from a guy when they have no better come-back but to humiliate a girl about her vagina or womb. I can't wait to leave school and be surrounded by adults so I never have to listen to this crap again.

'Boys our age have no idea,' Meg tells me. 'They're so immature it's painful. You don't get that with older guys, especially the ones who have been in relationships before.

They don't talk about periods like it's a disability, and they wash their dicks.' She takes a long, deep tug on her cigarette and stubs it out under her foot. 'Anyway, I have to go. See you in English on Thursday, and that's really cool you can make it on Saturday. Dean will be happy.'

She walks away. I want to scream after her, but I manage to contain myself.

I watch her walk. It's slow, relaxed, almost a swagger. She is probably stoned – she doesn't hide the fact she likes getting high. One time she came into English, sat next to me and said, 'I haven't slept in two days. I'm quite off my face. How are my pupils?'

Her pupils were massive and she looked like she had been attacked, but I told her she looked fine and she still answered every question Mr Frankel asked correctly and had obviously done all of her coursework. I don't know how she does it.

'Who is up for chicken?' bursts Pete, full of confidence and an incessant need to show off.

'Chicken is stupid,' I say. 'What is the point of driving at each other like that? You either pull away and look weak, or you keep going and die. It's such a stupid game, can't you just go and get pissed in town instead?'

'All right, mardy pants,' says Marcus. 'You should do it in your car, that would be funny. Actually, there are quite a few things I would like to do in your car. Like shag you.'

'In your dreams,' I say, walking off. Is that seriously how he expects to get sex?

I get to my car and throw in my bag. When I put the key in I turn and pump my foot, but nothing. It's failed again. Having to go back to Pete and Marcus and ask them to bump-start me is mortifying, but needs must.

'I'll do it for a squeeze of your tits,' says Pete.

'How about you just do it to be nice?' I say. They both nod and agree that's reason enough. They are not bad people, just clueless.

As they push my car down the road my engine eventually kicks in and I make it home in one piece, avoiding all major hills so I don't have to use my brakes. I love my car, but it really is a pile of crap.

3

Spice Up Your Life

Flo

Sitting in the window of Christies, Renée and I spend another two hours of our lives watching people we recognise walking up and down Guernsey High Street. It's the same faces every time. We know what time that blonde with the burnt orange cheeks leaves work at the hotel opposite, and when the sexy guy from the estate agents walks past on his way to the car park. We see random people with no schedule, very often from whom Renée has to hide because she snogged them the weekend before in The Monkey. Or girls she has to avoid because she got off with their boyfriend once. She does that sometimes. It sounds worse than it is. Renée is an opportunist. If something fun is staring her in the face she grabs it, not worrying about the consequences. She is a good person, sweet, loving, but capable of throwing her morals up in the air and not caring where they land. I know her well enough to know she's not a bad person. She just can't say no.

'Weird, isn't it?' I say. 'Our UCAS forms are being passed around to all those universities and people are judging us without ever having met us.'

She grunts and puts far too many chips in her mouth, even for her.

'You need to revise so you pass these exams, Renée. Or you won't get in and we won't have any chance of going to the same uni town. Can you imagine if you pass and I don't? That would be funny.'

'That would be unlikely,' she says, looking bored. 'Wait, weren't you going to do life-saving or something?'

'Yeah. I went once, but I hated how people can see you in the pool. There's that balcony and loads of boys gather on it while the lesson is on and laugh at all the girls' bodies. I felt way too self-conscious to save anyone's life. So I quit that. I hope I never come across anyone who's drowning. I'll feel so guilty watching them sink.'

Renée giggles. I love it when I make her laugh. She is the funny one, not me. It's always such an achievement when I crack a successful joke.

There is a pause in the conversation. A chance for me to tell her what's been happening in my life over the last few weeks, the side I haven't really told her about yet. The side I know she won't like.

'But I am going to keep going to church,' I say.

'Another "Flo fad"?' she says, undeterred and continuing to guzzle her fried potato like her life depends on it.

'This isn't a fad, Renée. Not this time.' I don't pick up another chip. I don't do anything to distract from what I am saying. I stare at her until she has no choice but to stop eating and listen to me.

'I believe in God. The last few weeks have been incredible for me,' I say. 'I go to church every Sunday, and to a friend's house every Thursday to pray and discuss the Bible. I am learning about Christianity, and it's changing my life.'

Silence.

A bit more silence, then . . .

'What *friend's* house?'

'No one's in particular . . . There are five of us. We take it in turns to meet at each other's houses on Thursday nights. Well, everyone's house except mine, because, well, you know my mum doesn't want me having people over. But we sit around, drink tea and talk about the Bible. We pray too, which at first I thought would be weird, but I really like it. One of us says what is on our mind and we hold hands and pray for them.'

'And then what happens? Does God appear floating on a cloud with a big white beard and tell you all how to live your lives?' she says, much more sarcastically than I was expecting.

'No, Renée, God doesn't just appear. But we all get some clarity and it helps us focus on what is important.'

'So, what is important then?'

'Our faith.'

'Oh right, of course.' She shrugs. 'Well, I give it a month.'

We sit there staring out of the window. Is she not even going to try to understand the positive effect this is having on my life? I am pleased for the break in tension when I see my friend Matt. I wave. Renée looks stunned, almost offended.

'Wait, who did you just wave at?' she asks, accusingly.

'Matt Richardson. He goes to my church.'

Her eyes start bulging, like I've taken all of my clothes off in front of her.

'Matt Richardson goes to church? But he smokes in the lay-by. And he's weird.'

'Well, you think that people who go to church are weird, don't you?' I say, giving her a moment to think about that. 'But he isn't, Matt is lovely. Ooh, he's coming in. And his mum is with him. Yay.'

Renée has gone stiff, like a scared cat. Only her eyes are darting around.

'Hi Matt, hi Mary,' I say as they come in. 'This is my best friend, Renée.'

Mary Richardson shakes Renée's stiff hand, and Matt just nods at her.

'We have come in for a hot chocolate,' says Mary. 'We will see you later on, though, Flo? Matt is happy to be having the group at our house tonight.'

'Lovely,' I say. 'Enjoy your hot chocolate. See you at seven.'

They go to the back of the café and we sit back down. I take the last chip from my bowl.

'What the hell just happened?' Renée asks, as if I just did something really inappropriate with Matt and his mum.

'What do you mean?'

'Matt? I'm just trying to get my head round it. *He* goes to church?'

'Yep. He doesn't want to get teased for believing in Jesus,

so he has this character that he plays at school that is not the Matt I know. We don't judge him for it, he just wants to fit in. But when he is with us he is so different, he's lovely. We respect that he doesn't want to be teased.'

'Who is this *we*?' asks Renée, clearly trying to deal with this conversation bit by bit. I know I am giving her a lot of new information all at once, so I hadn't expected her to take it on the chin.

'I told you . . . My friends and I – that *we*,' I say.

'Who are these people, exactly? You suddenly believe in God, you go to church? You have a load of new friends you pray with and Matt Richardson is lovely? Christ.'

Renée puts a fiver on the table and goes outside. I watch her walk to the other side of the road and light up a cigarette. Her arms are crossed and the hand holding the fag is up by her mouth. She is tapping her teeth with her fingers, lost in thought. It's what Renée does when she is trying to work something out. I don't go out to her. I will leave her to it, pay the bill and go home to get ready for tonight. Hopefully she will calm down soon.

Renée

I lie back on my bed staring at the ceiling. It's my favourite place, where I do most of my thinking. My bedroom was never somewhere I could relax before. Sharing a room with Nell was stressful. Not to mention the fact that my mother died in that room at Nana and Pop's house. But this room at Aunty Jo's is clean, mine, no history. It's where I can relax, chat to Mum without anyone hearing me.

However, right now, I feel quite stressed. Flo is religious. What is that about?

I am so used to Flo going through phases. Last year she got really into witchcraft. There is loads of it on Guernsey: a witches' circle that you are supposed to run around three times and make a wish, and in a bush somewhere there is a massive cauldron that has apparently been there for hundreds of years. Flo became obsessed with it all and got loads of books out from the library on local witchcraft. That phase was entertaining. We went on loads of adventures and it was exciting.

But then it turned into her being obsessed with magic. She saved up and bought a magic kit and started trying to teach herself how to do tricks. Every time I went round she would try a new one, but she was rubbish at it. Not to mention the fact that Flo is really shy, so any hobby that involves having an audience is never going to work. She would never have the guts to do it in front of anyone but me and Abi. When I told Aunty Jo about Flo and all of her fads she said, 'It's just her trying to work out who she is. She is looking for an identity. It's normal for girls your age. All of those teenagers walking around with pink hair and studs through their noses? Most of them will be plain as anything by the time they get to my age. They are just hiding behind an exterior while they work out what is going on inside their heads.'

As usual I am sure Aunty Jo is totally right, but Flo isn't like other teenagers. She is more grown-up than anybody else, more grounded, more secure, even though she is paranoid. She doesn't try to be anyone she isn't in the way that everyone else does. Sure, she has her fads, but she is fundamentally always just Flo. She doesn't show off or try to be cool to fit in – she just needs distracting, I think, from her morose thoughts about her dad. I know she thinks about him all the time and feels guilty about how sad he got before he had the heart attack. I know she feels that if she had made him happier it wouldn't have happened. So she gets obsessed with things to keep her mind off it. I understand it, I think it's actually quite admirable that she looks for things to perk herself up rather than wallow in the things that bring her down, but God? This is different. I don't like it. I just don't get it. And I have thought about it a lot.

When Pop died and I went to his funeral I thought about every word the vicar said. Pop spent his life grumbling about religion and how 'Holy Willies' were 'lunatics', but there he was being cremated in a church with a vicar saying he was off to be with God in heaven. Pop didn't even believe in heaven, so it all felt so insincere. I was very comfortable with the fact that Pop had gone and that was that. He was too – he told me that loads of times when he was dying. He didn't believe in heaven and didn't want to go there, even if there was a chance that he might see Mum when he got there, or that Nana would be up soon. His life was lived, it was time to say goodbye, he didn't want to carry on. I think the way religious people obsess about getting into heaven is just a romantic way of dealing with their fear of death. Who cares about what happens when we die? I say we should just focus on the life we live right now. If I go to heaven, bonus. If I don't, then I will have made the most of my time on earth. Religion just doesn't make sense to me. And like I said, I have thought about it a lot.

How can God be real when he allows people's mums and dads to die too young? When he makes people sick and tortures people? I see all of those children in Africa who are starving and covered in flies, and they die, all the time. If the bad stuff is the work of the devil, then the devil is winning and God's doing a really bad job. If God is real then I don't want anything to do with him – he doesn't seem like a very nice person. Constantly feeling like he has to prove to people that he is boss, always teaching people life lessons that are really no more than cruel abuses of his power. And what is he anyway? Is he the clouds? The stars? Is he the wind? Or is he an old man with a stick who watches over us? And why is He a he? I think children were once told a story about an old man in the sky and they believed it, like they did about Father Christmas. But it was so long before anyone worked out that this person doesn't really exist, so adults, not just children, believed these ridiculous stories, and then it was too late – it was embedded into human existence.

I need to distract Flo. As her best friend I have a duty to keep her mind off the things that upset her. I need to step up the fun, be naughty, keep life exciting. Remind her how far we have come in the last two years, really make her laugh. I go downstairs and get the phone book. I go straight to R.

Richardson. M

That must be them. I am sure Flo called Matt's mum Mary. I dial the number.

'Hello? Mary Richardson speaking.'

Bingo!

'Sorry about that,' I say to everyone as I come back in. 'Renée wants to meet me later.' Everyone smiles kindly like it doesn't matter. No one seems to think it's weird that she called me at Matt's house. But I suppose their focus is on other things.

'Carry on, Gordon,' says Sandra.

He gathers his thoughts and continues with what he was saying.

'Esau knew that to have the grace of God, he must forgive Jacob. So he did. God forgives those who trespass against evil, and to have his grace, we must do the same.'

Gordon is leading the group this week. Actually, he always leads the group. Not just because he is the oldest, but because he is obviously the most religious out of all of us. He knows every inch of the Bible and he is really good at making sense of it all. Today he is talking about forgiveness. I sit back down on the floor and try to get back into what he is saying, but Kerry interrupts.

'Does Renée believe?' she asks me.

They all, including Gordon, wait for my answer.

'She believes we're all mental,' I tell them and they laugh. This is nothing new to them.

'That's why I keep it quiet at school,' says Matt. 'I like going to the lay-by and joining in with everybody. If they knew about my relationship with God I would get teased for it. People don't get it, they don't like it.'

'You can't deny who you are,' offers Gordon, like a parent. 'If you are not honest about who you are then how will you ever accept yourself? I stopped caring about people having an issue with my faith a long time ago, and just surrounded myself with people who feel the same way. I never have to lie about who I am now.'

'To be fair, though,' says Kerry, 'it's quite hard to do that at school. You either fit in, or you don't. It takes guts to be different. I get why you want to keep it quiet there, Matt. You know who you are really.'

'I got teased at school,' interjects Sandra with a mouth full of biscuits.

'Why?' I ask. 'Because of God?'

'No,' she says, swallowing hard, 'because I'm fat. But I can hardly hide that, can I?'

We all laugh. There is something strangely endearing about a fat person who laughs at themselves.

'Shall we pray for Renée?' suggests Kerry.

I don't know what to say. The idea of it seems so weird.

'I don't think she needs praying for,' I say, hoping Kerry will move on, but instead she says, 'Everyone needs praying for. Tell us more about her.'

'She's fit,' says Matt. 'I see her in the lay-by all the time. She's really pretty, but a bit cool for school sometimes, and she flirts with everyone. Well, except me.' I can't help but laugh, although I seem to be the only one who thinks Renée being such a flirt is funny. But then my smile disappears. And without really planning what I am going to say, I start to describe my best friend.

'She is very special,' I say. 'Renée's mum died when she was seven and she doesn't really know her dad. Her sister moved to Spain to be with him a couple of years ago, but Renée would rather pretend he doesn't exist than deal with how much it would hurt her to see her dad. Renée's complicated. She is really confident, but a bit lost at the same time. It's like she doesn't really have any major ambition – like she just wants to have fun, you know, grab life by the horns? But deep down I think she'll be disappointed in herself if she doesn't achieve something. She's much more fragile than she lets on. So much of what she is about is wanting people to love her, because I think she feels like the person who loved her the most let her down. I don't mean that she blames her mum for dying, but if she was honest I think she would admit that the way she is a lot of the time is a result of what happened when she was seven. She basically watched her mum die. How can that not be the underlying thought behind everything you do?'

I stop talking and realise that if I let myself, I could cry for my friend, but I don't want the group to see Renée as sad, because she isn't. I feel odd about telling them such personal things about her when she isn't even here. It seems disloyal, but at the same time really nice for me to put Renée into words like that. She is very hard to define.

When I look at the others they are already holding hands. 'Come, join in,' says Kerry, urging me over. I take my seat and hold out my hands. When we are all connected Kerry starts. 'Dear Lord, please watch over Renée . . . '

If Renée could see this she would be really freaked out. But whether she likes it or not, I guess it can't do any harm to pray for her, can it?

No matter how many times I try, my car just won't start.
Chugchugchugchugchugchugchugchugchugchug

75

Urgh!

Chugchugchugchugchugchugchugchugchugchug

Then there is a tap on my window. 'Need a lift anywhere?' It's Gordon.

'So where am I taking you?' he asks when we are in his car.

'Tudor Falls. Renée said we should just meet there,' I tell him, knowing it's a weird place to be going. He asks why, but she wouldn't tell me so I can't tell him. I presume we are just going to a pub nearby.

Gordon pushes a tape into his stereo.

'We recorded this a few months ago,' he told me. 'I'm in a band. We're called The Trinity.'

I listen to the words, which are all about Jesus.

'It's a religious rock band,' Gordon confirms.

I don't know what to say about that, so I sit quietly and just listen to him sing along. The tunes are quite catchy, but although I have really embraced my faith in the last few weeks, I would still much rather listen to the Spice Girls.

I watch him drive. He has long, thin fingers, and his legs don't touch each other on his seat because he is so skinny.

'I am really enjoying having you in the group,' he says, ejecting his tape.

'Oh thank you, I'm enjoying it too. I can really be myself with you guys.' That's true. It's nice being with a group of people who are all comfortable with the fact that someone is bigger and better than all of us, so having a massive ego and trying to be the most important person is kind of pointless.

'I can always drive you on Thursdays if you like?' he then adds, which I take as flirting, which makes me blush. Thank goodness it's dark and he can't see.

'That would be really nice. Thanks.'

'And I have a gig on Saturday night, if you want to come?'

'You play gigs? Normal gigs? With this music?' I ask, wondering how The Trinity goes down in a Guernsey pub on a Saturday night.

'Ha, no. Maybe Guernsey isn't ready for that yet. It's in St James, and it's only promoted in churches, so everyone there will be Jesus-friendly. Come. I'll get you in free.'

I accept happily, despite my nerves. Already the fear of finding an outfit is crippling me.

'Well, here you go. Do you want me to just drop you here?' he says, pulling in next to the Tudor Falls gate. It's closed, and he looks confused. His headlights shine directly onto Renée who is sitting in the bushes. She has a saw in her hand. She couldn't look more like a murderer if she tried.

'Who's that?' says Gordon, squinting to see.

'That's Renée,' I tell him awkwardly.

'What is she doing?' He turns to me. 'Perhaps we should pray for her every week. She does look a bit strange.'

'Nah, she's fine, really. She, um, loves woodwork, that's what the saw is for. She obviously hasn't been home since school.'

What am I talking about? And what *is* that saw for?

'You can study woodwork at the grammar now?' he asks, surprised.

'Yeah, it's a module option. She loves it. She made all her own wardrobes.' OK, Flo, just stop talking. 'Anyway, I'd better go. Thanks for the lift.'

'No problem,' he says, pulling the tape out of the stereo.

'And have this – it will be more fun if you know the words at the gig. God bless.'

'God blugh . . . ' I say, chickening out of saying bless because it feels so silly to say it.

Gordon drives away and I turn to Renée.

'What are you doing?' I ask her, laughing.

'This is going to be FUN,' she says, walking towards the gate.

'Wait, what will be fun? What are we doing?' I ask, hoping she doesn't mean what I think she means.

'We're breaking into Tudor Falls,' she says, waving her saw. 'Come on.'

Renée

I am pumped. This is so exciting. Why haven't we ever done this before?

We crawl through the bushes to the side of the gate and jump out the other side. As we get further into the school grounds we see it: Tudor Falls. The building that, even still, knows more about us than anywhere else. It feels like home.

'It's creepy at night,' says Flo. But I don't feel that way. Nothing about this place scares me. I know it through and through.

'What if we get caught?' she asks.

'We won't,' I reassure her. 'There is no alarm and the caretaker left half an hour ago. I watched him go.'

'Well, how will we get in? And what on earth will we do when we get in there?' she asks. Two very valid questions.

'There was a window around the back of the changing rooms behind the gym that was always broken. I'll be amazed if it's been fixed. If it has then I will just smash a window. We are here now. Might as well go through with it.'

I am joking about smashing a window, but the look on Flo's face is priceless. 'And when we get in we will just have a look around, and I have an idea for something we can take as memorabilia. Right, let's do it.'

We walk down the side of the ugly concrete building like we did a thousand times for so many years. As we approach the gym I agree that it does feel creepy. The windows along the side of it allow us to see the swing bars and ropes we used to hang from. I imagine the echo of Miss Trunks' voice screaming at me to stop messing around. I feel a resounding sense of relief that my days of being screamed at by a fat, moody PE teacher are well and truly over.

As we get to the back of the gym to the window it looks closed, but that means nothing. It's always closed, which is why I think no one ever noticed that it was broken. But it doesn't lock. I know this because I broke it. I once had a panic attack trying to get a wasp out of the changing room. When I eventually managed to get it to fly out of the window I locked it so the wasp couldn't get back in. But I was so scared that I was brutal, and the lock snapped. I give the window a gentle push with my right hand and it opens. Brilliant. We are in.

The stale smell of sweat hits us when we wriggle our way through the window and land on the other side.

'Gross,' says Flo. 'It's like it's still our sweat we can smell. It's exactly the same. No wonder the window is still broken.

They have clearly never opened it.'

We get out of there quickly and find our way to the school's main foyer, where the headmistress Miss Grut's office is. Flo stands staring at the door.

'Come on, let's go to the staff room,' I say, but she doesn't move.

'That's where Miss Grut told me my dad had died. I still can't believe my mother allowed someone who hardly knew me to tell me something like that.'

I go over to her, stand between her and the door and hug her. I need her to hurry up. 'You've come such a long way since then, Flo. Come on, think about the good things, OK?'

'This place is full of bad memories, though, Renée. Why did you bring me here?'

Shit. It hadn't occurred to me that this might be traumatic for Flo. That is the room where she got told about her dad. Upstairs is the classroom where that bitch Sally told everyone about the worst thing I have ever done – have sex with Flo's brother. In fact, this entire building is full of haunting memories for Flo: death and being bullied and made to feel like shit by Sally. I need to turn this around, quick.

'But what about us? It's also where we became friends, isn't it? Without Tudor Falls we would never have met. Come on, Flo, maybe it's time to exorcise some demons. Let's go up to the science lab and our old classroom. No Sally, just us and our paper aeroplanes flying around with all our secrets on them. Shall we go up there? Pretend Mrs Suiter and her crazy eyes are staring at us?'

She nods and smiles. 'I guess this is a special place for our friendship.'

I grab her by the hand and pull her along behind me. The corridors are dark, but we know the way. The sucky scratchy sound that the double doors make as I push them open fills my head with images of me running when I was late for class. We creep up the stairs towards the science lab, and as I push the last set of double doors apart the familiar smell of vinegar and chemicals surrounds us. We hurry along to the end room where we used to have our class. There are a few green overalls hanging on the back of the door. We put them on and take our old seats.

'They've sandpapered away all of the writing on the desks. That's so boring,' I say, looking for something with a sharp point to correct their mistake. I find a biro and start etching an R on the bench.

'What are you doing?' hisses Flo. 'You can't do that. If our names are the only names on this bench they are going to know we broke in, aren't they?'

I throw the pen down and laugh. 'Wow. I mean, it just felt like the most natural thing in the world to do that.'

Flo looks at me like I'm crazy, then her face completely lights up, literally. The sound of a car engine seems unnaturally loud.

'SHIT!' we both say in a loud whisper. 'SHIT SHIT SHIT!' I run to the window and carefully look down. The caretaker's car is coming back towards the school. I feel sick. Flo is trembling so much I think I can hear her bones clank. We run to the back of the science lab, crouch behind the bench and wait.

'If he comes all the way up here we know he is looking for us,' says Flo. I know she is right. My heart is going nuts. I love being naughty, but I hate getting caught. We are full-on trespassing now. We have no right to be at Tudor Falls during the day, let alone at 10 p.m. at night. Please don't come up here, please, please. Then we hear the sucky scratchy sound of the double doors. He is getting closer.

'I'm so sorry,' I whisper to Flo. She takes a deep breath, as if she is going to stand up to hand herself in, and then we hear a woman giggle. It makes us both freeze. The door of the science lab swings open.

Flo

How the hell do I let Renée talk me into these things? I am not a violent person, but I could thump her so hard right now. Here we are, cowering at the back of a science lab in our old school wearing a random bit of our old school uniform. I mean, this is actually the kind of thing a mad person would do. I am not mad. Renée is, though – Renée is completely mental. Imagine if we get caught – this would be written about in the *Guernsey Globe* for sure. I would rather be teased about being a Jesus lover than be known for being a criminal. Oh God, why did I do this? I shut my eyes tight and clear my head. I say quietly, 'Please God, get me out of this. I'll be good, I promise.'

Renée, luckily, doesn't catch me doing it. We hold ourselves totally still. What will be will be. And then there is that giggle again. It becomes very clear that the caretaker is not alone.

'You bad boy, bringing me up here to take advantage of me,' says a woman's voice. It's familiar – deep and throaty – but I can't quite place it.

'Where are those overalls?' says the caretaker. I recognise his voice straight away. 'I left them up here on the door.'

'Never mind the overalls. Why hide this body?' says the woman's voice, and it comes to me in an instant. Renée and I look at each other and in perfect unison mouth, 'MISS TRUNKS?'

There is a clatter, the sound of rustling clothes, some aggressive kissing noises and then a 'I love those tits' from Mr Carter.

I can't believe this is happening. That horrible, fat, moody PE teacher having it away with the married caretaker and using the school as their sex den? Eeeeewwwwwww. I become aware that the overall I am wearing was intended for her so he could dress her up for his kinky game. I am desperate to take it off – have they used it before? Gross. I start to unwrap it but Renée stops me. She is right, I cannot move. We cannot get caught.

'Be my naughty little school girl. My naughty little bitch,' he says, panting into what I presume, and hope, is her mouth.

'Bitch?' Renée and I mouth at each other. Seriously, God? I think. Is this your idea of helping me out?

The next five minutes involve a lot of banging around, pumping, slapping sounds and a few squelches that I try not to absorb into my memory. Miss Trunks certainly sounds like she loves it and Mr Carter keeps saying how big and strong he is, how she wants him, how he is inside of her. I am so glad I haven't just eaten.

When they are done, giggling to each other like baddies from a cartoon, they leave. We wait. Totally still, barely breathing until we hear the caretaker's car engine start and his headlights have passed all the way up the school drive. The relief pours over us like a tidal wave. We both jump up and hop around like we have been caught by sprinklers. I instinctively brush my body with my hands as if getting those two off me. I feel covered in grime, like I'll never be able to escape this dirty feeling. I want a shower, a five-hour power shower. With bleach.

'THAT was THE most DISTURBING thing I have EVER EVER heard!' says Renée, both hands leaning on the work bench as if she has just run up the stairs and is out of breath.

'I just can't believe it,' I say, sounding as shocked as I am. 'I just can't believe that just happened. I can't believe Miss Trunks is a sexual human being. I can't believe the first time I was ever in the same room as actual real-life sex it was . . . that. I can't believe we just witnessed that. I will never be the same again. I'll never be able to have sex now.'

Renée nods in agreement. Still panting a bit. She looks wrecked.

Then the giggles start, uncontrollable belly laughs that come with hysteria and shock. We are lost in it, laughing so hard my tummy struggles to support it. Like catching a sneeze, I almost have to wait for the chance to engage my stomach muscles so I can let out the roar of laughter that has come right up from my feet. We don't know what we are laughing for. Is it the relief? The shock? THE SQUELCH?

I didn't know laughter like this was possible in this building.

It's a good twenty minutes before we have the ability to use our legs again to leave. Constant dramatic exhalations and 'oh my Gods' show that the giggles might have stopped but we are by no means over it. As we get to the door of the science lab Renée stops and tells me to wait.

'What?' I say, feeling like we have used up all of our lives in this situation and just need to leave.

'Let's take it,' she says, her trademark naughty grin creeping across her face.

'Take what?' I ask, baffled.

'Him!'

I follow her eyes to the corner of the room.

'No!' I say firmly. 'No, bloody, way!'

Renée

I'm not going to lie. Trying to get an adult-sized human skeleton into a Fiat 126 doesn't come without its challenges. In the end we decided it should sit in the front. Partly because trying to get it in the back might have caused a fibula to fly off, and partly because, out of respect, we thought he had the right to have the best seat in the car.

'What shall we call him?' I ask Flo, as I drive them both back to my house.

'Ricky?' she says.

'That's so random.'

'It just feels right.'

Ricky it is.

'Hello, Ricky,' I say. 'Let's get you home.'

With Ricky wrapped around me like a drunk boyfriend we

step into my living room. The TV is on, Aunty Jo is out and Nana is in her chair, fast asleep with a blanket over her knees. I left her here nearly three hours ago. I know that was awful, but I have never once seen her wake up of her own accord when she falls asleep in front of the telly at night. So the chance of it happening while I was out was small, and luckily I was right, but I am glad Aunty Jo didn't come home early and find out. She's on a date with a guy she met by the meat counter in Safeway. Apparently they bonded over how they like their lamb chops burnt to a crisp. God knows how they got onto that, but then adults have weird conversations when they are out and about making chit-chat.

'Get the coat stand from the hallway,' I tell Flo. 'We can loop a scarf around his shoulders and hang him from it.'

Flo obediently trots off and comes back dragging the coat stand. We weave the scarf in and amongst his bones and position him so he looks happy. 'Now what?' asks Flo. 'Shall we dress him up?'

Flo is being surprisingly relaxed about all this. Usually when I make her do something naughty she panics and the fear of getting caught makes her jumpy and weird, but right now she is completely up for this. I like it – this is how I always want Flo to be.

'You're keen,' I say, with a surprised smile.

'I realised something tonight. People are bad. Mean. People do awful things to people. Mr Carter is a married man, and there he was in a school science lab trying to dress the horrible Miss Trunks up as a school girl so he could have weird sex with her behind his wife's back. On the science benches, where a young girl will sit tomorrow and have no idea that just hours before the spot where she puts her jotter was the spot where Miss Trunks' squelchy, sweaty bum was being slapped by her fancy man. It's not right.'

'No, it isn't,' I say, even though I have kissed loads of people's boyfriends and think the idea of sex in a science lab is quite fun. But not with Miss Trunks and Mr Carter. I shake my head to get the image out.

'I spend so much of my time feeling guilty, insecure and paranoid that I am messing up, when really, I am a good person,' says Flo. 'I don't do things that hurt other people. I don't lie or cheat, or sleep with people I shouldn't sleep with. Why am I the one who feels so crap about myself all the time? Other people seem to coast through life being shits to people and getting away with it.'

It's hard to know what to say. I essentially do all of those things, and in the past have even done them to Flo. I don't think I am a bad person either, but I could easily fall into the category of the people she has just described.

'My church friends don't do things like that either. They are good people too. So many people lack basic morals. It's depressing.'

'Hmmm,' I murmur, trying to sound like I get it.

To be honest, this is all getting a bit intense. And I don't want Flo thinking about her church friends when she is with me. If I am honest, I don't want her thinking about her church friends at all. In the nicest possible way I need to move her on from this philosophical moment she is having. Right now, my grandma is snoring on an armchair next to us, and there is a human skeleton hanging from a coat stand in my living room. Forget the flippant morals of the human race, we have a skeleton to dress, and I want to have fun.

'I've had an idea' I say next, running out of the room. Hopefully this will take Flo's mind off God.

I come back with a huge plastic bag in my arms. Nana is awake.

'What a lovely man,' she says, smiling at me as I walk in. I shoot a look at Flo. She nods, confirming that Nana is talking about Ricky.

'What's in the bag?' asks Flo.

Now, I have a tendency to think beyond the 'bleedin' obvious' (as Pop used to say) when people are in need of a spot of light comical relief, but I can honestly say this is one of the best ever strokes of comedy genius that I have ever had. I open the plastic bag and pull out Aunty Jo's wedding dress. Despite her being generally quite stylish, this eighties frock looks like someone threw up a Mr Whippy. Layers of billowing crushed ivory silk, silly bows and tacky embroidery. How she ever thought this was a good idea I will never know.

'Ahhh, a wedding,' says Nana, looking thrilled. 'Who is getting married?'

'Ricky,' says Flo. 'Ricky and Renée.'

I feed Ricky's feet through the dress and pull it up over his shoulders. 'Quick, go and get the camera from the drawer in the kitchen,' I tell Flo. 'We must document this special day properly.'

She comes back and snaps away. I have pulled Nana's armchair round so it is next to me and put the flowery head piece on her that was also in the plastic bag. I have linked Ricky's arm through mine and I flutter my eyelids as if blissfully in love. I think Nana thinks it's genuinely a wedding, she is so happy and smiley.

'OK, look at your new husband,' instructs Flo. I turn to Ricky and gaze lovingly into his eye sockets. 'Do you, Renée, take Ricky to be your lawful wedded husband?'

'I do,' I say, wistfully.

'Do you, Ricky, take Renée to be your lawful wedded wife?'

I say 'I do' like a really bad ventriloquist and tug on the neck of the dress so Ricky nods.

'I now pronounce you hu—' But before she can finish her pronouncement the distinctive noise of a sharp gasp stops her going any further.

I turn to see Aunty Jo, her arms crossed angrily over her chest, glaring at me and Ricky and Flo.

'What do you think you're doing, Renée?'

I have never seen her look so mad. I immediately feel like a total fool.

The atmosphere in the room turns really cold. Aunty Jo is standing in the doorway. And it looks like she might cry.

'I got married in that,' she says, quietly, glossing over the fact that a skeleton is wearing the dress. 'You think it's funny that my marriage didn't work out?'

This is awful. Aunty Jo never gets like this.

'We are not making fun of you,' I say awkwardly. 'I . . . I just thought it would be funny to dress Ricky up . . . '

But no amount of explanation can make what is going on seem like normal behaviour. Aunty Jo sighs heavily, shakes her head at me and then walks away. Flo and I hear her bedroom door close. I feel terrible.

Flo gives me an 'Oh shit' look.

'I'll get the dress off him and wait in your room,' she says, starting to undress Ricky.

Meanwhile, Nana is still sitting there, staring at Ricky, as though everything is completely normal.

'Come on, Nana,' I say, 'let's get you to bed.'

'Did she change her mind?' she asks.

'Did who change her mind, Nana?'

'Your wife?'

'Something like that, Nana,' I tell her.

I guide her to her room, see her into bed and give her a kiss goodnight. 'Sweet dreams, Nana. I love you,' I say as I shut the door. Only a few years ago she did the same to me.

'Aunty Jo,' I say, tapping on her door and opening it gently. 'Can I come in?'

She is lying face down on the bed, a pillow over her head. It's the kind of position I would lie in, and for second I imagine her as a teenager. Mum's little sister.

'I'm really sorry I upset you. I didn't mean to.' I say, sitting next to her.

She pulls away the pillow and rolls over. She hasn't been crying, but she looks exhausted and stressed. She sighs again, but looks less mad.

'I know you didn't, Renée. I just saw my wedding dress and you both laughing at it and seeing it played out in front of me reminded me of how much of a fool I feel for getting married.

I should have thrown my dress away, but I just couldn't.'

'You're not a fool. You only got divorced, loads of people get divorced. Mum and Dad got divorced, quite a few people in my class have divorced parents. It's normal.'

She puts her hands on her face and groans.

'But I never wanted to get divorced, Renée. In front of all my family and friends I stood up in that stupid bloody dress and told the man I loved that I would spend the rest of my life with him. He said the same, but I knew, I knew he didn't mean it like I did, but I still went ahead with it.'

'Do you really think he didn't love you?'

'He loved me, of course, but not the way he should have. I think he thought I would do, but that he had always hoped for something better. He used to point out all of my faults, which put me in my shell. He thought he was being helpful, telling me how to better myself all the time, but all that meant is that I got smaller and smaller until I was completely invisible to him and he wanted to be with somebody else.'

'He sounds really mean. I didn't realise Uncle Andrew was like that,' I say, shocked and quite upset that I was ever nice to him.

'It's subtle. He was perfectly nice to me on a daily basis, but he obviously wanted me to be a different person so found it hard to hide that,' she says, sitting up. 'People don't have to think each other is perfect in a relationship, but if you want to change someone you have to be gentle, filter it through in other ways, not just constant criticism; offer advice and encourage, not slam them for being who they are. I lost my confidence and he let me drown, never once trying to save me.' She drops her head a little. 'I'd have divorced me too. And now look at me. Forty-four, single and loveless. I will almost definitely never have a child of my own because I married the wrong man. That dress is a symbol of all of that. It's hard to see any humour in it, you know?'

I feel so sad. I never thought Aunty Jo had struggled like this – she has always been so private about her marriage. But of course it broke down because it was awful – why else would it?

'Sorry,' she says, and blows her nose with a tissue that's in her hand. 'I shouldn't tell you these things. You have dealt with enough, and you don't need to hear about sad old spinsters with tragic love lives.'

I put my arm around her.

'To be fair, Aunty Jo,' I tell her, 'you're not the one who just married a dead transvestite.'

That makes her laugh.

'How was your date?' I ask, hoping it went well.

She rolls her eyes.

'Turns out the only thing we have in common is the way we like our lamb chops cooked. By the end of dinner I wanted to burn him to a crisp, to be honest. Ah well, I'm sure Mr Right is out there somewhere. Thanks, darling. You go to bed, I'll be all right.'

'Sure?'

'Sure!'

Just as I get to my bedroom door, Aunty Jo calls out, 'Renée?'

'Yeah?'

'That skeleton won't stay in the lounge, will it?'

I turn and smile. 'Night, Aunty Jo. Sleep tight.'

92

4

Too Much

Flo

Lying back on my bed I listen to the lyrics of Gordon's music. The chorus of one song is:

Christ, you are my smile
Christ, you are my sight
Christ, you are my every thought
Christ, I love your might.

How can Christ be your smile? I try not to overthink it and attempt to lose myself in the music. I want to have learned all of the words in time for the gig tonight. I have an hour before I have to leave. That would be a pretty cool thing to do. Cool in a going-to-a-God-themed-rock-concert kind of way.

I haven't been able to stop thinking about Gordon since

Thursday. I know he isn't the sexiest guy ever, but there is something about him I really fancy. I think it's just how well he knows himself, how self-assured he seems. How comfortable he is with his faith. Comfortable enough to stand on stage in front of a room full of people and sing songs about it. I can't imagine doing anything like that. I haven't even told my own mother I am religious, let alone an entire ticket-paying audience. I want to have as much conviction – I want to feel what he feels and believe the way that he does. I close my eyes.

'Dear God,' I say quietly, 'thank you for the last few weeks. I've really enjoyed getting to know you. I'm not sure I am at the stage of head banging to rock songs about you, but I am not really the kind of person who would head bang to rock songs anyway, so please don't be offended. I will give it a go though, I promise. I just wanted to tell you that I have been feeling better about Dad. I still miss him every day of course, but I think I feel less guilty, or at least more understanding about the fact there was nothing I could have done to stop his heart attack. And I can breathe through those moments where I miss him so much I could cry. I just focus on him and smile and somehow the tears just don't come. That is when I feel you the most, when I find a way to stop the tears. It's like you dry them up for me. I have created a voice for you in my head – I think you would like it. It's quite deep and slow, and soothing. It wouldn't work on anyone else – a human might come across as a bit creepy – but for you, it works. I think you might have sent me a message the other night at Tudor Falls? I thought making me sit through the sex with Miss Trunks and Mr Carter was a really odd way to do it, but I did get your message. You showed me that I am a good person, didn't you? You reminded me how other people do bad things, how they lie, how they cheat, and that my guilt and my issues with myself really are not based on anything I have actually done. That is right, isn't it? That is the lesson you wanted me to learn? So thank you, God. I . . .'

'Who on earth are you talking to?' asks Mum. She is inside my room. I can feel the heat coming off her. What do I do? Do I tell her, or do I pretend I am learning something for school? She looks exasperated with me, but then she often is. This is who I am now. I must be strong.

'I was talking to God.'

'What?'

'God. I've been going to church for weeks.'

She looks confused.

'God?'

'Yes, God. Do you believe in God, Mum?'

'No, I do not. You know I don't go to church.'

'Well, I do. Did you want anything?'

I can't quite gauge her reaction. It's impossible to tell whether she's angry, or surprised, or possibly even frightened. She just keeps staring at me lying on the bed, her eyes scanning me up and down. Then it's almost as if she remembers what she is here for.

'I need you to babysit Abi tonight. I have been asked out.'

'By a man?' I ask.

'Yes, by a man, Flo. I wouldn't have thought I will be late.'

I very rarely say no to my mother. Partly because I rarely need to, because I hardly have the world's most kicking social life, but mostly because even though our conversations might make us sound like two people who are virtual strangers to each other, we actually get on better than ever now, and I want it to stay that way. My life is now a juggling act of trying to keep her on a level so she doesn't have a nervous breakdown – something I am aware she could have at any given moment if she had the opportunity – and I worry that saying no to her will put us back to where we were even two years ago. She hated me, and I hated her. These days we can just about stomach each other. It's a vast improvement. But tonight I am not available, and she is going to have to be OK with that.

'Sorry, Mum, I can't. I have a date too.'

'You have a what?' She looks flabbergasted, which doesn't do much for my ego. 'Is Renée going?'

'No, Mum. I love Renée, but I wouldn't take her on a date with me.'

Mum is obviously having trouble processing almost everything I have laid on her since she walked into my room.

'What is this music?' she asks.

'It's The Trinity. My boyfriend is the lead singer.'

She stands, staring at me, like I'm an alien. I close my eyes again. I feel so stupid for calling Gordon my boyfriend. I don't know where that came from. Maybe God made me say it. I keep my eyes shut and hold my breath, hoping that my face doesn't turn bright pink.

Mum continues to stare at me for a bit, and then she gives a small shrug.

'Well, I guess I could ask my date to come here,' she says at last, before she leaves the room.

I am shocked at two things. One is the fact that my mother is being so reasonable, when she is not a reasonable woman. And the other is that I just called Gordon my boyfriend, which he isn't. Yet. Did Mum and I just have some weird mother–daughter chat about boys by accident? I suppose I shouldn't question any of it. Just go with it.

Now, what on earth am I going to wear?

I struggle with outfits at the best of times, usually opting for the same thing of black trousers and either a black T-shirt with sparkly bits on the shoulders and my denim jacket, or I borrow something of Renée's. She has got some really nice stuff now that her aunty Jo takes her shopping. Mum, on the other hand, still thinks that as long as my naked body is hidden I don't need anything new. Even though we are not broke, not after Dad's life insurance came through, and she now works full-time on reception at an insurance firm, she still can't bring herself to give me money. My job helps – I get thirty-two quid a week from Smellies, and much more when I work the holidays, so I am doing OK after Easter. But since shelling out to fix my car, buying new shoes and paying Mum back for the magic kit she agreed to buy for me last year – as long as I paid back every penny – I am not left with much.

I put on my black trousers and the black T-shirt with sparkly shoulders. It's fine. The Trinity gig will hardly be the fashion party of the year, will it?

As I arrive at St James, a large church just above town that is now a concert hall, there are a lot of people outside standing in front of a big poster on the wall – with Gordon's face, a crucifix and the band name and logo (another crucifix with a hand around it) and the words *The Trinity, TONIGHT!*

People are smoking. There doesn't seem to be anyone over about twenty-five, and at a glance it looks like any other group of young people hanging around outside a gig. Kerry runs over to me.

'Flo!' she shouts to get my attention. 'Here, have some of this before we go in. They are checking bags.'

She passes me a big bottle of cider and I have a sip. I didn't realise she drank. On Thursdays we just have tea and whatever high-sugar snacks Sandra brings, and we all munch away happily as we talk through whatever part of the Bible we are discussing that week. But no one has ever mentioned booze. I think I just presumed they didn't drink. Kerry definitely seems a bit pissed tonight, though. It doesn't take much to make me drunk, and I want to have a clear head tonight, so I just have a sip and hand her back the bottle.

'I am so glad you came,' she says, hugging me affectionately and kissing my cheek. It's the kind of lingering hug that feels like more than just a hello, and more like a needy thank you. 'I wanted to invite you myself, but wasn't sure if you were ready for a load of rocking Christians all in the same room. It can be a bit full on.'

'I'm ready. I'm looking forward to it. Gordon said he would get me in for free.'

'He did? Wow, he is usually quite tight with the tickets.' Kerry doesn't look too impressed. 'Shall we go in?'

As Gordon promised, my name is on the door, but Kerry's isn't. I feel bad about that, but I guess I have to get used to that, if he is going to be my boyfriend. He can't get everyone free entry, can he? I feel cool for the first time in my life.

The room is huge, very churchy in shape but not churchy in how it's decorated. There is a big balcony with lots of seats and there are already lots of people up there, but down in the main bit in front of the stage people are just standing and waiting for the band to come on.

I had no idea there were so many young people on Guernsey who are into God. It's like another world. I recognise some of them from other years in school – a couple of girls from Tudor Falls, for instance – and some from just being out and about. I should probably say hello or something, but I am happy sticking with Kerry, and I am keeping my eyes open for Gordon. I wonder if he'll come and see me before he goes on stage?

'I learned all the words to Gordon's songs,' I tell Kerry. 'Well, most of them.'

'Wow, you're like their groupie,' Kerry says in a weirdly unfriendly tone. 'Free entry, memorising his lyrics . . . Next you'll want to get together with the lead singer.' She isn't looking at me, but her body language has completely changed. I could take a guess that Kerry is being so off with me because maybe she's jealous because she fancies Gordon and wants him all to herself. But I like Kerry and I don't want to go there. So instead I pretend I haven't noticed and allow myself to fantasise about going out with a guy like Gordon. I wonder if he's ever had sex.

I'm eighteen and a virgin. I'm all right with that – I was never in a hurry to lose my virginity before – but I definitely feel like I might be ready, if I find the right guy. Since going to church and meeting with the group I feel a bit more confident, like I am really part of something. I don't feel like the saddest person in the room when I am with these people. Like I can trust them. The thing that put me off sex in the past was the idea of a boy getting to know my body before he gets to know me. I overhear so many conversations in the common room where the boys are telling their mates about the girls they got off with, or making fun of girls' fannies and boobs in some way. It makes me really paranoid. I would rather be a virgin so no one could make those jokes about me than have sex with someone just because I feel I should, and open myself up to that kind of humiliation. The last time I let a boy put his hands in my knickers I forgot I had my period and he told everyone. I'm still not really over it, wondering who knows and who is laughing about me. The thought of someone laughing about how I smell down there or how weird they find my body is too much for me. It's horrible. A guy like Gordon wouldn't laugh and joke about a girl's body, I can tell.

And there's something else – I've never been hugely sexual, and I don't think I'm normal. Renée is so comfortable with being sexual with guys that it's kind of intimidating to talk about it with her, because she doesn't understand how it feels to not want to share yourself with anyone else. She also masturbates a lot, but I rarely do. I try it sometimes but nothing really happens and I just feel embarrassed. I am generally of the mindset that if you are doing something that makes you feel embarrassed when you are on your own, you should probably just stop.

The lights dim a bit and people start clapping. Then Gordon and his band walk out onto the stage. He looks different. There is something about his aura that has changed. He looks a bit like a rock star. I get a fizz of excitement.

'Thank you all for coming,' Gordon says into the microphone. Everyone cheers, and it is obvious that the vast majority, if not all of the people in this room, are already fans of the band. I have only ever been to one gig. It was when Sister Sledge performed at Beau Sejour, the local leisure centre, about ten years ago. It was full of screaming girls under the age of twelve. This is full of seventeen- to twenty-five-year-olds with bottles of beer in their hands. It is not the same kind of gig. Still, I like the atmosphere. When I've been to a few more Trinity gigs I'll probably know how to behave at them. For the moment I am just being an observer.

'I am Gordon Macintyre.' There is a cheer from the crowd. 'We are The Trinity. Welcome to St James – is everybody ready to tell the big man how we feel?'

Everyone in the room shouts yes. It makes me jump. Gordon looks so sexy up on stage. I don't feel cool, and these people aren't supposed to be the cool kids, but here, in their world, they kind of are. The band kicks off, a sea of hands go into the air. Most people shut their eyes and drop their heads, which seems a bit odd when you have come to watch a band. I soon pick up the words to the first song.

'I will follow you, Jesus, I will follow you, Jesus, I will follow you, the Lord.'

The song pretty much just repeats that line with various levels of intensity as it goes on. Everyone, absolutely everyone, is singing along, totally consumed, from the second it starts. They are lost in it. Arms in the air, eyes closed, praying. Gordon looks up the whole time, staying focused on a spot on the ceiling at the back of the room as if he is talking directly to it. In church it's so quiet that people are subdued in the way they pray. Here it's different. This is dramatic worship, loud, expressive, confident. I am standing in the middle of it feeling for the first time since I started coming to church that I don't fit in. This is all a bit much for me. I don't get it. I look at Kerry. Her head is facing up but her eyes are closed. Her arms are in the air and she is limp. She knows all of the words, and there is even a tear rolling down her cheek. I want to be like that – I want to feel that too. I close my eyes, put my arms in the air and reach up. I try to imagine God above me, watching me, grateful for my love. I want to feel my faith tingling in my fingertips as I connect with him and everyone around me in this other dimension they have all gone into. But I can't. I feel silly and self-conscious. Insincere and unconfident. I want to ask Kerry to teach me, but I don't want to disturb her. Plus she's been sending out hostile signals for the past half an hour, ever since we talked about Gordon. Right now, her mind is somewhere else.

I lower my arms and I push my way gently through the crowd to the toilets. People smile as I brush past them, but hardly anyone opens their eyes. I lock myself in a cubicle and wait until it's all over. I feel a bit ridiculous and glad I didn't wear anything more fancy.

An hour and a half later the music has stopped. Quite a few people have come into the toilets, knocked on my cubicle door to ask if whoever is in here is OK, and I have shouted back 'food poisoning' far too many times. It's time to brave the outside world again, but I feel so silly. Checking my face for dislodged make-up, I wash my hands and make my way back out to the main hall. There are around half the people in there, and in the middle I see Gordon, his band mates and Kerry all chatting with bottles of beer. I'm certain I have the indentation of a toilet seat on my bum and thighs from sitting on it for so long. Thank God for clothes.

'There you are!' says Kerry, cheerily. She's definitely changed her tune. For some reason this annoys me.

'You were so great,' I say, looking to Gordon.

'You're here? I was looking for you but couldn't see you,' he says, but I am not sure I believe him. When I saw him on stage he only looked up.

'I thought you'd left.' Kerry seems friendly now. I can't work out why she's changed moods so quickly. Maybe she's got her period or something.

'No, I didn't leave. I just went closer to the front. I was down there, by the stage, about two from the front. It was brilliant,' I lie.

'I knew you would get it it,' says Gordon. 'You are the kind of person wh—'

'Does anyone want to come to the pub?' Kerry says, cutting through him. 'It's only 10 p.m. We could get a few in before last orders?'

'Not me,' says Gordon. 'I'm done after all that singing. Do you need a lift home, Flo?'

'Aren't you coming to the pub, Flo?' Kerry sounds like she really wants me to come. What is up with her?

'Well . . .'

'Flo looks like she needs some quiet time,' says Gordon,

looking right into my eyes.

Oh my God, it's so obvious that he fancies me. I pray my face doesn't change colour and just say, 'Thanks, that would be great.'

I hug Kerry goodbye, but she's back to being a bit frosty. 'See you at church in the morning?' I ask.

She half nods, half shrugs and turns back to the group quickly.

Leaving me and Gordon alone together.

Driving along in Gordon's car he plays a tape of his own band, and sings along with a song that he wrote. It's one where the chorus manages to rhyme the word *might* with *Christ*. It isn't very good. He turns down the volume to speak to me. 'Thanks for coming tonight, Flo. It means a lot to me that you were there.'

'It does?' I say, wishing I had just said thank you. 'It does?' sounds so pathetic and under-confident.

'Yes, it does. To see that you are serious about worship. It's not just for Sunday church services and a weekly Bible meeting. It's for all days, with all people. The band gives us a new way to pray, a more youthful connection with God. I feel so close to him when I am on stage singing these songs.'

'Everyone was really into it,' I say, unsure of what the right thing to say is. I want to impress him, and make him feel like I understood tonight. Even though I spent most of it pretending to have diarrhoea in the toilet. 'It's a different thing, though, isn't it? When the band and the audience are all singing about the same person. Like when you hear a song usually, like, I dunno, when Toni Braxton sings 'Unbreak My Heart', she has

104

a picture of someone in her head that she wrote the song about and is singing it to. When people listen to it some of them have a person that they can think about too, but some people don't. It doesn't mean they can't enjoy the song, but it doesn't mean as much to them as it does to the people who can visualise something. But with your music, on a night like tonight, everyone is thinking about the same person, Christ, so everyone is involved with what you are singing. You, I mean, *we* were all sharing the exact same experience,' I say, wishing I would just shut up.

'Flo, you are so right. That was spot on. I knew you would see it.'

We drive up the road to my house. 'This is me,' I say, and he slows down. I undo my seatbelt slowly, not really knowing if I am supposed to get out or stay put. Will we kiss?

He turns off the engine and shifts to face me.

'I can take you further into faith than you ever imagined, Flo,' he says, looking me right in the eye. I wonder if this is meant as a euphemism, and hope a kiss is on its way. 'I think God has asked me to embrace you.'

'He has?' I say, shyly. 'Embrace me, then?'

I reach my arms across to his seat and try to hug him, but his arms don't move. He just lets my head rest on his chest and he pats it. 'There, there,' he says.

There, there?

I look up at him. Maybe he's being gentlemanly and respectful. Should I show him that I want him by kissing him first? My lips are underneath his – it's obvious what I want. And then he does – he kisses me. Just off my mouth and no tongues, but it was still a kiss. Then he pushes me gently back over to my side of the car. Was that good? I really can't tell, but I want to say all of the right things, so I lie.

'That made my fingers tingle,' I say, hoping he wants to do it again, this time properly.

He smiles. 'I know that feeling well. It's how I feel when I sing my songs to God. It's like he runs through me.'

I want to tell him that God had nothing to do with it, but I think better of it. I don't want to ruin the moment, or to be rude. I liked the kiss, kind of. It was better than no kiss. And in a way I much preferred it to the horrid, sloppy, beer-smelling snogs I have had in The Monkey on the nights when I have got so drunk I thought I might as well.

'Goodnight, Flo,' he says.

'Goodnight, Gordon.'

I get out of the car, and before he sets off he pushes in his tape again and turns up the volume. I can hear him singing along to it as his car drives out of sight.

It wasn't exactly a passionate encounter, but it's a start.

Is it possible that I, Flo forever-the-virgin Parrot, have a boyfriend?

As I walk into the house I hear noises coming from the kitchen. Mum is still up and she obviously isn't alone. Her date must still be here. Usually I do everything I can to avoid anything to do with her love life, but her laughter stops me going upstairs. Because my mum never laughs, at least not like she is now. It's not the fake, sexually charged laughter I have heard her do around boyfriends before, but more natural-sounding.

106

'Mum?' I say, opening the door.

'Flo, you're home.' She looks a bit flushed. 'This is Arthur.'

Usually when meeting Mum's blokes I brace myself to have either my hand shaken or my cheek slobbed on, but when I look at Arthur, I am happy to have my hand shaken by him. He is tall, with dark brown hair, small glasses and a nice suit.

'Hello, Flo,' he says. 'Lovely to meet you. Are you desperate to get to bed or would you like to join us for a glass of wine?'

Mum and I both look at each other strangely. Us? Have a glass of wine together? That's the weirdest thing I have ever heard. But before I have the chance to say no he has poured me one and put it in my hand. I then do something I thought I would never do – I sit up until the early hours of the morning laughing and joking with my mother and her really nice new boyfriend.

Renée

I call my boss at about 5 p.m. to say I have been feeling sick all day, and I can't work tonight. He says, 'Sorry to hear that,' but in an annoyed voice, which means he knows I am lying, but nothing is going to stop me from going to see Dean's play.

I drive into the youth theatre car park and see Meg and Dean standing outside smoking. I quickly put some make-up on using my rear-view mirror. I'm wearing blue jeans with a light blue jumper, a black bomber jacket and Converse boots. I think I look quite cool. Getting out of my car I am careful to look like I don't care if Dean is watching, but I do, I do – I want him to be watching me so much. As I walk over to them my heart is pounding, but I am determined to be confident and not show my nerves. I have been such a nervous idiot around so many boys, but this time I am not doing it. Cool, I am going to be cool.

'Hi guys, you all right?' I say, like I have been coming to plays on Saturday nights for years.

'Renée, you came,' says Meg, in her usual laid-back and slightly stoned way. 'This is Dean. You guys haven't met properly yet, have you?'

Rather than shake my hand, Dean kisses me softly on the cheek. 'I feel like I know you,' he says. 'I've seen you around for years.'

Flattered, I feel I should reciprocate. 'Me too. I love your work. I read the piece you wrote in the *Globe* about the controversial right turn up in Torteval. I thought it was really great.'

'Ha! That's very kind. But I hardly get to flex my creative muscles in the *Globe*. Guernsey is hardly the epicentre of gripping news stories. Tonight, though, you'll get to see some of my real work, the stuff that makes me tick. You should go in – curtain up in five. I'll see you two afterwards.'

'He's so nice,' I say to Meg as we take our seats.

'Yup, and such a talented writer. His stuff is really deep.' The lights go down and two actors come on. They are half dressed and look intense. Meg turns to me and smiles as if I am about to experience something wonderful. I see Dean sitting down in the front row. He must have seen this a thousand times, if he wrote it. I am excited. Coming to the theatre feels so grown-up.

I spend the next hour and a half trying to follow what's going on, but I just don't get it. Two men, speaking in low monotone voices, using modern language but really long and complicated words that nobody in real life would ever use. The basic plot is that one of the men slept with the other man's wife, and that they are trying to work out who should have her. In the end they decide they both should but just not let on to her that they know. I didn't realise it was possible to feel so sorry for a fictional character that wasn't even in the play. That poor wife. When the lights go up, the thirty-two (I counted) people in the audience clap, and we go outside. Dean is already at the door and people are congratulating him as they leave.

'That was so great,' drawls Meg, hugging him languidly.

'Thanks, babe.' Dean looks to me. 'What did you think, Renée?' he asks.

'It was really interesting,' I reply, taking note from Aunty Jo, who told me that if you can't think of anything to say about an artist's work, you should always just say it was 'interesting'.

Dean obviously likes what I said. He smiles and I see his eyes start to wander down my body. I try not to look too ecstatic about that. Which I am.

'Shall we go into town?' suggests Meg, who seems oblivious to the electricity between me and Dean. 'I think you probably want to get drunk, don't you, Dean?'

'I certainly do. The Ship and Crown?'

'Oh no, I can't go there tonight,' I say quickly. 'I am supposed to be working and I did a sicky. I probably shouldn't go into town at all. If I get spotted I'll lose my job. You guys go.'

Dean frowns.

'I tell you what, fuck The Ship. Why don't you two come

back to mine? I have loads of booze, and some other treats. It'll be fun.'

A very high-pitched and annoyingly girly squeal is released into my brain, but I manage to contain it and just say, 'Cool. Sounds great!'

'And I think we should go in your car, Renée. Looks like a laugh.'

We all pile in. Dean in the front, Meg in the back. Dean laughs at the way I have to pour anti-freeze into the engine before we can leave, and I warn them that there is a good chance they'll have to bump-start me if the engine doesn't start. But it's OK. My little car is on my side for once.

'I live in the Canishers,' he says, 'just above The Royal Hotel. On the far side of town. There should be plenty of parking down there.' He pushes in the tape that's currently poking out of my stereo and I prepare to cringe, but Dean laughs when he realises it's the Spice Girls.

'GIRL POWER!' I shout, though neither of them shout it back. I must remember that I can't act the way I do with Flo with everyone else.

When we arrive at Dean's flat it is obvious that Meg is a regular there. She goes straight into the kitchen to get some drinks from the fridge. As she clanks around getting glasses, Dean and I are left alone in the living room.

'So I liked your dance the other night. They were some moves you were throwing.'

'It was the routine Madonna does in the 'Papa Don't Preach' video. I wanted to put on a bit of a show for you.' I laugh, letting him know I don't take myself at all seriously.

'Well, you succeeded. I couldn't stop thinking about you after that.'

'Really? I saw you at the bar with Meg and thought you guys were together.'

Dean shakes his head.

'No, we haven't been together for a long time. Just friends.'

Meg comes in with three glasses and a bottle of white wine. I am turning things over in my head. Dean and Meg are exes? I wonder what Dean means by 'a long time'? Why has Meg never mentioned it? I take a glass of wine from Meg and decide not to bring it up right now. I can't be jealous yet – nothing has even happened between us.

'Where's the gear?' Meg asks Dean.

'You know where it is. It's where it always is.' She goes over to a little wooden box on the mantelpiece and gets out a big bag of weed.

Dean's flat is small. It's nice, though – the few things he has are interesting. A glass coffee table that has thick, hand-made wooden legs. A deep-green sofa, loads and loads of books on shelves around the room and tons of VHS along the skirting boards. There are photos of him and various people all over the walls – it is very obvious that he is well travelled.

'You live on your own?' I ask him.

'Essentially, yes,' he answers. 'Come on, I'll show you around.' We leave Meg skinning up on the sofa; she doesn't even look up when we leave the room. Down a short corridor he shows me his bathroom and then leads me into his bedroom. The bed is very low, a wooden frame that slightly elevates a double mattress from the floor, but not by much. It smells of essential oils, cedar and neroli, I think. I recognise them from the selections Flo has given me as birthday and Christmas presents. She gets a good staff discount from Smellies.

'Here, sit here,' says Dean, sitting down on his bed and patting the spot next to him. I feel slightly odd about the fact we left Meg in the living room, but she looked pretty happy, just her and her weed. I sit down next to him. I feel inexplicably horny. He is so fit. Dark hair, nice deep-brown eyes, big eyebrows, a good nose, thick lips, strong jaw. Handsome. Interesting. Arty. Writery. He oozes experience and knowledge. He makes me want to know stuff, about everything.

'I'd like to see those later,' he says, pointing at my breasts. From anyone else this would have sounded like the sleaziest line of all time. Somehow from him, it just sounds sexy.

'What about now?' I catch myself saying in a whisper. I don't want him to see me as too young. I am eighteen – I am an adult. I need to act like one now.

The light is off in the bedroom, but the hall light gives enough that my skin will look nice.

'What about Meg?' I say as I start to take off my top.

'Don't worry about her. Meg's happy sitting in there for hours just smoking and reading my books. She's fine.'

My jumper is now on my lap. Dean wets his lips.

'I knew they'd be good,' he says, stroking my left boob with his hand. Then he leans forward and licks my nipple. The lick turns into a suck, and then his teeth gently nibble it. Then he nibbles a bit too hard and I jump from the pain.

'Gently, please,' I say, and he goes to lick the other one.

It's hard to tell guys when they do something you don't

like, but I have learned that you have to. Or they just don't know. Imagine a world full of men who have never been told by women about the things we don't like? It would be awful. So we have to tell them – it's our duty. It feels good that I am grown-up enough to say it to someone like Dean.

'Dean?' comes Meg's voice from the living room. 'Dean, do you want some of this?'

'Yes babe,' he shouts back, then whispers to me, 'Stay here tonight,' before he gets up and heads back into the living room, leaving me on the bed.

I pull my jumper back on and take the opportunity to use his bathroom, which is right opposite the bedroom in the narrow hall. It's pretty clean, for a guy's bathroom. There are quite a few products – shaving foam, aftershave, a selection of deodorants. His toothbrush is in its holder and the lid of the toothpaste is on. I open a little cupboard to the right of the sink, just to see what else he likes to spray himself with, but amongst an impressive selection of aftershaves is a bottle of women's deodorant, some mascara and a box of tampons.

Meg's? Who else's could they be?

'He isn't your boyfriend, Renée,' I say at my reflection. 'Stay calm.'

I have a wee, and head back into the living room.

'What the fuck?' are my first words when I see their faces up against each other's. Kissing. So blatantly. How was I so . . . And then I see the jet of smoke shooting from Meg's mouth. She's giving him a blow back. I feel like a total fool. 'Sorry, I thought you were . . . '

'Come and sit here,' says Dean, patting the sofa next to him.

It's obvious that he and Meg are both so stoned they haven't even noticed what I said. He passes me the spliff.

I take it, but I know it's probably a bad idea. I haven't smoked much pot but when I have I've spun out, felt sick, had what I have come to know as a 'whitey'. It's when the world stops spinning and you spin instead, and then everything stops, and you can't even move. So I do that, then I go into a coma. It's nothing dangerous, just a heavy drug-induced sleep, but I am always really jealous of the people who smoke loads and get the giggles, or do what Meg seems to do and get cleverer and cleverer the more she smokes. Regardless of my experience, I take the spliff. After one drag, I know it was a bad idea. Everything goes hazy. I pass out.

My eyelids can barely block the light of the morning. It feels like a torch is being shone right into my face. Before I open my eyes I assess myself. I am lying down, I am under a cover. I don't have socks on. As I move I feel that the duvet is directly on my skin. My hands reveal I have my bra and knickers on but nothing else. My eyes ping open. Where am I?

I'm in Dean's bedroom, in his bed, and he is asleep next to me. His back is facing me. It's a nice back, smooth. There is a tattoo on his left shoulder – it looks like a Chinese symbol or something like that. His boxer shorts are Calvin Klein. He looks nice, but this is so weird. I have been in bed with boys I don't know before, but at least I remembered getting into bed with them. I don't even know if we had sex or not, but I have my pants on so I presume not. I try to get out of bed quietly. I don't want to wake him and I really need the loo.

'Good morning, sleepy head,' he says, turning over.

Damn it!

'Morning,' I say, sitting on the edge of his bed. 'It goes without saying I can't remember anything.'

He laughs. 'Don't worry, you were perfectly dignified. You just fell asleep after about four drags. It's Meg's fault, she packs so much in when she skins up. I carried you to bed at about midnight. I took off your clothes, but I didn't think you would appreciate me stripping you naked.'

I try not to dwell on the thought of being carried. I hope I wasn't too heavy.

'Thank you,' I say, meaning it. A lot of boys wouldn't have missed an opportunity like that. I feel a little less ashamed knowing that I wasn't spreadeagled in front of him.

'I'm just going to pop to the loo,' I say, getting up and slipping on his T-shirt.

'Don't be long. I am not such a good boy when the girl I fancy is awake.'

In the bathroom I feel very aware that he is still lying only feet away from where the toilet is and that the flat is silent. I am desperate for a poo. I run the cold tap, lay a few sheets of loo roll in the toilet and sit down, leaning forward so I can reach the running water. I flap my hand under the tap so it sounds like I am washing my hands and hope to God I manage to do this without any embarrassing noises.

I get through it and feel oddly proud of myself. I have never actually spent the night at a boy's house before. An entirely plop-free poo was surprisingly easy to achieve. It's a skill I feel glad I have acquired. After a quick spray of the women's

115

deodorant I found in the cupboard last night, I think I dealt with that really well. When I come back into the bedroom, Meg is sitting on his bed. I'm relieved to see that she's wearing a big dressing gown that comes down to her ankles. It must be Dean's, but at least she's not naked.

'Morning,' she says, as if her being there is completely normal. Then she runs into the bathroom with a towel and I take it upon myself to close the bedroom door.

'Meg stayed, then?' I ask him, trying not to sound jealous.

'Yeah, she stays a lot. Freshened up?' he asks, moving the conversation on too quickly.

'Yup,' I say as I get back into bed and under the covers. I shiver a little as my body gets back to the temperature it was more happy with. Dean's hands are on me straight away.

'I can have you now that you are awake,' he says, laughing. He lifts up my T-shirt and I wriggle out of it, even though the daylight is so bright, and his curtains are thin. I tell myself to be grown-up about my body, and not insecure. But I don't like my white flesh in raw daylight, the way all of my imperfections glow.

'I love stretch marks,' he says, running his hand over my hip. I want to scream and tell him to get off. I hate them so much. But here we are, and I have no choice but for him to see them. I can either get all insecure about it, or take what he says as what he means.

'What do you like about them?' I ask, uncomfortably.

'What they do to the skin. How they make it feel so soft and delicate. A symbol of how you have grown. Like the rings of a tree. Your own private markings, unique to you. Nature's own tattoo.'

'Anyone'd know you were a writer,' I tell him, unable to keep the wariness out of my voice. 'That was pretty convincing.'

Come on, Renée, I think to myself. Your body could be worse. Relax.

'Renée. I have seen you around for so long, and I always thought how sexy you are,' he says. 'I came into The Ship once and you were wearing this low-cut black top and your jeans. Every time you turned around I would look at your bum. You didn't even know I was watching you.'

'I knew,' I say. 'I always knew. I was watching you too.'

'Can I make love to you?' he says softly, even though he is tugging at my knickers. Relaxed as I have convinced myself to feel, it takes every shred of will power I have not to burst out laughing. No one has ever said 'make love' to me before. Do people really say that? I thought it was just in the movies. I guess this is what happens when you sleep with people in their twenties. I embrace it, it's kind of sexy, once you get over the shock of it. So I tell him he can.

We start slowly. Instantly I realise how unsensual the sex I have had before has been. Dean takes his time, he seems to understand every part of me already. Like he's seen it before. He asks me what I want, and I am brave enough to tell him, even though it feels embarrassing to ask for it out loud. He tells me what he likes too – he likes to be in my mouth. He makes noises that make me feel good about what I'm doing. He is firm with me but not rough. His penis tastes faintly of soap.

'Wow,' I say when we are done. 'Just. Wow.'

'You liked that?'

'Liked it? I, I . . .' I try not to sound too experienced. Even though I have slept with a few people now, I realise I have certainly never 'made love'.

'I loved it,' is all I can think of to say.

'Plenty more where that came from,' he tells me. 'Open the window there, will you? It's got a bit stuffy in here.'

'Sure,' I say, throwing aside the covers. I don't even think about the fact that I am naked and that I have to stand up in front of him, I just do it, I stand up, and with that comes a fart noise so loud that I fall to my knees on the floor.

'IT WAS MY VAGINA, NOT MY BUM!' are the first words that fly from my lips. Then I grab a pillow and put it over my face as I press my head into the floor. 'I don't know where that came from. I'm so sorry.'

I am so mortified. A fanny fart? That has never happened to me before – not an unintentional one anyway. I used to make Mum laugh by doing them on purpose when I was about five, but Pop used to get so angry that Mum told me I should probably stop doing them and think of some other jokes. This one was so loud, so powerful. The kind of fart you do when you have been having to hold one in for hours. The volume and the speed at which it shot out of me was such a shock. Why was there no warning?

'Renée?' he says to the pillow covering my head. 'It's OK.'

'But it isn't OK. It is everything but OK.' I just almost took off from an explosion from my own vagina. Nothing about this is OK.

'Seriously, get over it. I'm the one who pumped you full of air.'

This is true. It wasn't like that would have happened if he hadn't 'made love' to me. I remain still for a few more seconds. My bum facing up, my face down, too scared to move in case my fanny is plotting more evil.

'Seriously, Renée, just open the window. Sex is all about weird noises and smells. I don't care about that stuff. All I care about is that we do it.'

Smells? I daren't even ask what he means by that.

'Has anyone ever fanny farted in front of you before?' I ask, then I quickly add, 'Actually, please don't answer that.'

Dean laughs.

'I'll go make us some tea. Get back into bed.'

I wait until he has left the room before I move. Standing up, I jog up and down to get any last puffs of air out and I put on my underwear and clothes. I grab my bag, which is by the bed, and leave the bedroom.

'I actually have to go,' I tell him and Meg, who are both in the kitchen. She is wearing one of his T-shirts and her pants. It feels weird.

'What, no tea?' he asks, looking genuinely surprised.

'No, I promised my aunty I would help her with some things at home. I do have to go. Thanks for such a great night, and congratulations on the play. It really was great.'

'Ahhh, is she all embarrassed about her farty sound?' Dean says, coming over to comfort me.

'Dean? Please, Meg will hear you.'

'She doesn't care about that stuff. Come on, babe, don't go. We can stay in bed all day?'

'No, I really do have to go. But thanks, I had fun,' I say,

walking to the front door.

'All right. I suppose I'd better crack on with the piece I have to write anyway,' Dean says.

'Anything interesting?' I ask, genuinely curious.

'Not really. Some idiot stole the skeleton from the science lab at Tudor Falls. The paper has asked me to do a piece on immature school antics.'

I do a good job of keeping my expression totally blank as I say, 'That's kind of funny.' I am hoping Meg and Dean will see it the same way.

'Yeah, funny if you think stealing something that educates children is a good thing.'

That wipes the smile off my face.

'Just kidding,' Dean smiles. 'It's hilarious, but whoever did it is going to be in a lot of shit when they're caught. Trespassing and theft? That's pretty bad.'

Shit. I smile tightly, hoping he's exaggerating, and then spot a pen on the table.

'I'll give you my number then?' I suggest, writing it down on the corner of an Indian takeaway menu. 'Call me, if you like,' I say as casually as I can. 'I'd like that.' I go over and give him an awkward kiss goodbye. 'See you at school, Meg.'

'Bye, babe,' says Meg.

I leave, wondering what the two of them will do now. Will they spend the day together? Will he tell her about my fanny fart? Boys talk, I know that much. Bugger it, I just have to suck it up.

Bad choice of words.

'So did you two kiss?' asks Kerry as soon as we get to church. She slips in next to me on my regular pew. I wonder if I should tell her or not. Will it cause a weird atmosphere on Thursday nights? But I am in church, I can't lie in here.

'Yes, but just a little one,' I tell her. I can't wipe the big stupid smile off my face.

'So is Gordon your boyfriend now?'

'No. I mean, we only kissed once. But maybe. I think I would like that. He is great, isn't he?'

'I suppose so.' Kelly turns to face forward and I see something sag a bit in her expression.

The vicar comes in, and Kerry focuses on him in such a way that I can tell she doesn't want the conversation to carry on. I subtly scan the church with my eyes looking for Gordon, bearing in mind that he could be behind me. Renée says you should always behave like the boy you fancy is watching you, in case he is. I know when she has a crush on someone because everything she does is like a performance. I could never be quite like that, but I do pull my tummy in and stick my neck out so I don't have a double chin, just in case.

Then I see the back of Gordon's head. He is about four rows in front of me with his head down. He is praying. I think there is a good chance that he is always praying. I know that most people in the church are thinking about God while they are here, but Gordon always looks like his mind has left his body and he is actually with God somewhere. Sitting on a cloud, having a chat. He is so connected to him, I wonder if I will ever get like that. I think I'd like to, I think it would probably be quite nice. To get off earth for a bit and go float around somewhere else chatting away to the Lord.

At the end of the service Kerry and I go outside, but rather than talk to me she walks off with Matt. I don't know what I keep doing to offend her, but I need to try to sort it out. There's a tap on my shoulder.

'Flo.' It's Gordon. 'You get to sleep all right after I dropped you home?'

I want to tell him the truth. That I lay awake for hours thinking about him, that I fancy the pants off him, that I wished he had kissed me properly. But I don't, of course. I tell him I got to sleep just fine.

'What are you doing now?' he asks. I presume he wants to do something so I tell him, 'Nothing,' but then he says he is going to play an acoustic set to the parents and kids at Sunday school, and I wish I had made up something exciting that I was doing too. Even though there is nothing. He scrunches up his eyes a bit as he looks over my shoulder. I think he might be seeing who is about before he gives me a proper kiss, but instead he says, 'Isn't that your friend?'

When I turn I see the unmistakable silhouette of Renée walking down the high street towards us. What is she doing out and about in town this early on a Sunday morning? She has the most spectacular bed hair, and black make-up is smudged under her eyes.

'Is she talking to herself?' remarks Gordon.

'Renée!' I call. She looks up and is obviously as surprised to see me as I am her.

'Flo, what are you doing in town?' she says, coming closer. 'Oh my God, did you pull?'

I feel myself recoil as she says it. She couldn't have picked a worse time to say something like that. Without looking at Gordon, I say, 'No, of course not. I've been to church. This is Gordon, my, er, friend from church.' My heart thumps with relief that I managed to stop myself saying boyfriend.

'I thought it might be your boyfriend,' Renée says, with that look in her eyes that tells me she is winding me up.

'No. Friend,' I say firmly. 'This is my friend Gordon.' My face explodes with blood vessels and I turn the most fluorescent shade of pink imaginable.

'Flo, you're blushing,' says Renée, teasingly.

I screw my lips up and tilt my head to ask her to please stop embarrassing me. When people comment on my blushing it just gets worse.

'Ah, you're the one who's into woodwork?' says Gordon. I shake my head at Renée, begging her not to react. 'God bless you, I have heard a lot about you,' he goes on, not really taking any part in mine and Renée's exchange.

'God bless you too,' she says back, sarcastically.

'Anyway, didn't you have to get off?' I say to Gordon, needing this moment to end.

'Yes, see you later.' He leans forward and kisses me on the cheek. 'Bye bye,' he says, as he walks away.

'Bye bye,' Renée mimics. 'Is he even human?' she asks, when he is out of ear shot.

'Yes, he is human. And he's really nice actually. Really interesting.'

'Flo, he talks like he swallowed a Bible.'

'All he said was "God bless".'

'I know! Who says that under the age of fifty?'

'OK, well, I like him. Really like him.' I can't hide my disappointment at how mean she is being.

'Oh Flo, I'm sorry. Come on, I'm starving. Let's go for breakfast and you can tell me all about Bible Boy.'

'RENÉE!'

She throws her arms around me and leads me back up the high street. She smells weird.

'. . . And then he kissed me,' I tell her, taking a bite of my egg sandwich.

'Hang on, back up the truck. There is a rock band that sings songs just about Jesus?' she asks.

'Yes. It's Gordon's band. They're called The Trinity. They had a gig at St James. It was really good.'

'Yeah?' She orders some ketchup and doesn't look up at me before she starts to speak again.

'So, you're serious about all this God shit then, are you?'

'It's not shit, Renée. I didn't invent Christianity, it's not some random fad a few people have told me about. It's religion, faith – it's always been a part of our lives in some way. I just haven't chosen to embrace it until now.'

'What is it you like about it?' she says, sounding totally unconvinced.

'It gives me something to believe in. It takes the pressure off me. It gives me guidance, when I am doubting how I should behave. It makes me feel like Dad is within my reach, like I am still connected to him in some way. It makes me feel part of a community, a group of people I can be myself with. But mostly it's made me feel less guilty, less self-consumed. Less like I am all I have in the entire world and like when the time comes that I leave home and leave this island I won't be completely on my own. It just makes me feel better, Renée. Is that so bad?'

'I guess not.'

Her passive tone infuriates me. Why is her way OK, but my way is not?

'So who were you with last night then?' I ask. Let's hear how she is living her life, if her way is so much better.

'I pulled that guy, Dean, the writer. The one we saw in The Monkey, you know?'

'Yeah, I know. You've fancied him for ages.'

'Yup, and we got on really well. I just left his before I bumped into you.'

'Did you have sex?'

'Of course we had sex, Flo. That's what normal people do when they pull and stay the night together.'

'Was it good sex?'

'Amazing.'

She goes quiet. She always does when we talk about sex. She thinks I will mention the fact she slept with my brother, but I will never mention that ever again. I made that decision at the time. But she isn't telling me something, I know.

'Are you all right, Renée?' I press. 'Did something happen?'

She doesn't say anything, but I know she is thinking about whatever it is.

'Flo?' she asks, after a few minutes. 'You know how I get really embarrassed buying tampons?'

125

'Yeah. For someone as confident as you I find it really bizarre.'

'Well, I think I have another fear.' She puts down her knife and fork and takes a gulp of orange juice. 'Would you mind going to Boots and getting me the morning-after pill?'

She *has* to be joking.

Renée

I have had to wait until today, Monday, to get the morning-after pill as everywhere was shut yesterday. So in our lunch hour we drive down to town in Flo's car. Apparently you have seventy-two hours before it's ineffective. I know I should have made Dean put on a condom, but he didn't mention it and I didn't want to ruin the moment. He is so experienced I did think he might do the withdrawal technique, but he didn't. Anyway, it's fine. Loads of people take the morning-after pill – the only annoying part is that you have to go into the chemist and ask for it. Apparently they ask you loads of questions and that kind of thing really freaks me out. I have still never, at the age of eighteen, bought a packet of tampons myself. Aunty Jo gets them for me and leaves them in the bathroom downstairs. We never talk about it – she just keeps the supply topped up and I help myself. I know I will have to do it one day, but until then I am putting it off. Flo, on the other hand, is good at this stuff.

'They will probably ask you when you had sex, if he was your boyfriend and if you used a condom,' I tell Flo. I know this because I overheard two girls in the toilets talking about what happened to them when they needed it last term. 'Tell them it was yesterday morning, that you are in a long-term relationship and that the condom broke, OK?'

'Oh Renée, do it yourself. This is crazy,' she says. I agree, it's crazy, but I am who I am.

'Please, Flo. It's the one thing I can't do. It makes me so embarrassed, I don't know why. Please?' I hold out thirty quid.

'For God's sake,' she hisses, and snatches the money out of my hand and storms into Boots. I wait outside and light a fag.

After a few minutes, I see Meg walking up the high street.

'Hey, Renée,' she says, noticing me. 'I was just on my way to Dean's house. Wanna come?'

My heart plummets. He didn't call last night, and I thought he might. Does he not want to see how I am? To say he had fun?

'He invited you over?' I ask.

'Oh, I don't bother waiting for an invitation. He is chilled about me being there.'

I really want to ask her what the deal is with that and why she is always at his place, and tell her how I think it's a bit weird that she stayed there when he was in bed with me in the other room, when Flo comes out and pushes the thirty quid quite aggressively into my shoulder.

'Sorry, Renée. I can't tell lies,' she says, looking a bit upset. 'Get your own pills.' Then she notices Meg and goes into slow motion. As pissed off as Flo is, she obviously feels terrible for sharing my secret with someone she doesn't even know. 'Shit, sorry,' she says, looking at me.

'You need the morning-after pill?' says Meg, twigging. 'Don't bother with the thirty quid. Here.' She reaches into her bag and pulls out a pack of contraceptive pills. 'Just take all of these.

I used to do it all the time before I went on the pill. A whole month's worth of pills is the same as the morning-after pill. You might feel a bit sick, but it works. I don't have a baby, do I? Here, you can have these.'

'Er . . . thanks,' I say, taking the pills.

'No problem. See you later?'

She walks off, slowly. Flo and I watch her until she is far enough away that she won't hear us.

'You know you can't take those, don't you?' Flo says, frowning. 'I don't think it's the same thing as the morning-after pill . . .'

'They're better than nothing, though. I'd rather take these than have a kid. It will be fine, Meg said she used to do it all the time.'

'Renée, I don't think Meg knows what she –'

But before Flo has finished I have popped most of the pills into the palm of my hand and am preparing to swallow them.

'I can't watch this. You can get the bus back up to school,' says Flo as she turns and walks towards the car park.

I don't follow her. The last thing I want right now is a guilt trip about the way I live my life. I swallow the pills and start walking up towards school. Despite what Flo thinks, I'm sure Meg knows what she is talking about.

' . . . I think I am dying,' I say to Aunty Jo as I am bent double in the phone box trying not to be sick.

'Where are you?'

'At the top of the Grange, in a phone box. I'm going to be so sick.'

128

'Walk over to the medical practice. It's just there up to the left, you know it. Go in there, ask to see someone and I will be there in ten.'

I pretty much crawl up to the doctor's surgery. How could I have been so stupid to take all those pills? How could Meg have been so relaxed about it? Surely this happened to her too? I think all these things as I run behind a car in the surgery car park and puke up so hard I worry if my stomach is going to follow. I can see some undigested pills in my sick. By the time Aunty Jo's car pulls up I am sitting on the step feeling a lot better. She sits down next to me. We can see Nana in the car, smiling and listening to the radio. I tell Aunty Jo what I did.

'That was stupid,' she tells me. But of course I already know that. 'I think it's probably about time you went on the pill, if you are sleeping with this guy, Dean.'

I have no idea if I am going out with Dean or not, but I think Aunty Jo is right.

'Go in and make an appointment,' she tells me. 'You might get one now if you're lucky. Nana and I can wait here for you.'

At reception, I ask if there are any appointments.

'Do you want a male or a female doctor?' the receptionist asks really loudly. I feel like everyone is looking at me, judging me, like they all know I had unprotected sex.

'Female, please,' I whisper.

'Right. Well, Dr Burrington can see you now. We have had a cancellation.'

I go stiff.

'Dr Burrington? Is there anyone else?'

'Not female, I'm afraid. Take a seat, please. She won't be long.'

I sit in the waiting area. There is an old man with warts all over his nose, a pregnant woman who looks like she is about to burst and a young girl in a Tudor Falls uniform with her mum. I would run away, but I think I'm going to puke again.

I know Dr Burrington well. She is the doctor who looked after Mum the whole way through her illness. I haven't seen her since I was a little girl, since Mum was dying. I feel seven years old again, but here I am about to ask her to put me on the pill.

Then she calls my name. Her voice catapults me back eleven years to the time I was listening at the door as she told Mum that she would do her best to make her as comfortable as she could during the 'last few weeks'. Her face sends a flood of emotion through me that launches me forward until I find myself hugging her. I feel the eyes of the receptionist on me, wondering what the hell I think I am doing.

'Come through, Renée,' says Dr Burrington. 'It's lovely to see you after all these years.'

It isn't long before I am talking at 100 miles an hour, trying to fill her in on the last eleven years. She knew bits and bobs; that Pop had died, and that Nell had moved to Spain and that I am now living with Aunty Jo.

'Word travels on a small island like this,' she says, 'and I always ask people I know who know your family, just to keep updated. I was terribly fond of your mother.'

'It's so good to see you,' I tell her. 'Mum really liked you, I know she did.' I realise that I've got tears coming, and I try to hold them back.

'We were friends too, that's for sure. She was a wonderful

woman. You look just like her.'

That's my favourite thing anyone ever says to me.

Dr Burrington looks at her watch. 'Sorry, Renée. I have been so enjoying talking to you, but I have another appointment waiting.' She smiles. 'So, tell me, what am I seeing you for today?'

This is where I have to be brave. I think about Mum, and how she never knew me as a woman, but how I am one now. I am a woman. I am eighteen, I have sex and periods and boyfriends. I drive a car that I bought with my own money, I help take care of Nana now, I am doing A levels and soon I will be leaving Guernsey and going off to have my new adventures. I have to stop feeling like a little girl when it comes to my body.

'I need the morning-after pill today, and I would like to go on the pill too,' I tell Dr Burrington. 'I had unprotected sex yesterday morning, and a friend told me to take a whole packet of contraceptive pills because I was too nervous to buy the morning-after pill. They made me sick, and now I am worried I might be pregnant.'

She smiles again, a reassuring smile, as if she has heard all this before.

'If I had a pound for every girl your age who thinks that works, I would be much richer than I am. No one can keep twenty-plus pills down for long. When is your next period due?' she asks.

'Soon, like any day.' I am surprised how easily I feel I can offer that information.

'Well, the chances of you getting pregnant at this point in your cycle are unlikely, but still possible. I will give you the

131

morning-after pill just in case. I'll also give you six months' worth of pills. We can see how you get on with those, all right?'

'Thank you.'

Dr Burrington talks me through when and how I should take the pills. What to do if I miss one and what to do if I don't want to have a period once month. It sounds great.

'I'll be so in control of my own body,' I say.

She laughs. 'There is a reason the pill changed women's lives back in the sixties. It gave us a freedom that women never thought was possible, but you still have to be careful. This doesn't protect from STDs, so my advice is that you still use condoms until you are in a serious relationship.'

'All right,' I say, knowing that I probably won't.

I take the prescription and go to leave. As I get to the door I turn back to her.

'Dr Burrington?'

'Yes, Renée.'

'Thanks for trying to save my mum. I was too young to thank you at the time, but I know now that you made those last few weeks as good as they could be.'

'It was my privilege to be there for her, Renée. Come see me any time, OK?'

'I will.'

I leave. As promised, Aunty Jo and Nana are waiting for me in the car outside.

'All sorted?' asks Aunty Jo.

'All sorted,' I tell her.

She drives me back to school.

5

Move Over

Flo

'Today, let's talk about forgiveness,' says Gordon, sitting on his dad's armchair in his living room. The rest of us are sitting on the floor looking up at him like his disciples.

We meet here almost every week now. Gordon likes to lead the sessions. He wants to preach, he tells me. It's quite full on, but then what he says makes sense, and I guess someone has to do it to keep passing on the message of God. From a girlfriend (which I think I am) perspective, though, it's a little intimidating. We have spent more and more time together over the last few weeks, but it's rare that he manages to have a conversation without bringing it back to God in some way. As much as I am really enjoying my faith, I find it a bit much.

'Bear with each other and forgive whatever grievances you may have against one another. Forgive as the Lord forgave you,' he reads. 'Colossians 3:13. We all have people who challenge the Lord's command for us to forgive, but we must trust his instruction and forgive by our faith, not follow what our instinct often tells us. That to forgive is weakness, to forgive is as if to approve of someone else's wrongdoing. Forgiveness is neither of these things, forgiveness is acceptance in accordance with the grace of God.'

There is something about this particular session that is troubling me. Forgiveness is a big deal for me. I am eighteen years old and have had to forgive people my whole life. Mum, Julian, Renée, myself. Even Dad, in a funny kind of way. I had to forgive him for letting himself go, for giving up on himself so badly, for getting so stressed, so unfit that his heart killed him as he was taking the rubbish out one Thursday afternoon. I think I have done a good job in forgiving all of these people in my life. But obviously there is one person who makes the concept of forgiveness more challenging for me. The person who is the reason I still doubt myself every day, even though Renée and the church have tried to teach me that I shouldn't. I don't think I could ever – no matter how much my relationship with Christ depended on it – forgive Sally de Putron.

Gordon continues, 'Not forgiving makes you the prisoner in your own life. Our happiness in ourselves comes from our relationship with God, not with others around us. God is the only one capable of unconditional love. If we take our eye off him, we run the risk of being privy to the corruption of others. Remain focused on God, and remain focused on faith. God knows that all humans are weak, he knows we cannot expect to rely solely on the good of others.'

'But what if there is no point in forgiving?' I ask my boyfriend, the preacher. 'What if the person who hurt you so much isn't in your life any more? Rather than forgiving them, you just move on, and don't bother with them any more. Why forgive people when you can just cut them out?' I take a Rice Krispie cake from the tupperware box being waved under my nose by Sandra. Her eyes are fixed on Gordon's face, almost trance-like, but even so she is still managing to channel her need for sugar.

'You may never see a person in the flesh again, but that doesn't mean that anger doesn't burn inside of you every day,' Gordon says. 'If there is someone you haven't forgiven can you tell me honestly that you don't think about them all the time? As they have gone off to live their life, who is left with the damage of what they did?'

He is right, which is annoying. I am left with the damage, all of it. Sally is off being a mum to the baby who obviously loves her and I still think about the way she used to make me feel every single day.

'Forgiveness is for you, not a right of passage for them. If you never see them again they will never know you have forgiven them. It doesn't matter to them, it matters for you. Let's pray.'

We all put a hand on someone else's shoulder or knee. Gordon leads us through a prayer.

'Dear Lord, we ask you to guide us in our quest to forgive those who do us wrong. To lead us from temptation and away from evil. Help us understand those who are good and those who are bad. We ask you to trust that we have devoted our lives to you, and that with your grace we can keep peace within ourselves. We are your servants, Lord. Christ sacrificed himself for us and for that we owe our lives. Amen.'

'Amen,' we all say quietly.

'Is it all right with everyone if I have the last one?'

'Yes, Sandra.'

In the car on the way home Gordon is playing me the new song that he has recorded.

'Gordon?' I say, but he doesn't hear. 'Gordon?' Again, he doesn't respond. 'GORDON!' I shout, pressing eject.

'What? What, Flo? We were just getting to the best bit.'

'Gordon, would you like to come into my house when you drop me home?'

'Sorry, Flo. I need to get home. I have to write a sermon for the kids at Sunday school this week.'

'OK,' I say quietly. 'It's just that we have been going out with each other for nearly a month now. You pick me up and take me to our Bible meetings, and to church, and you have got me in free to a few of your gigs now, which is really sweet. But don't you think it's time you came into my house? Or that we did something else, just us, maybe that isn't about church?'

I think I worded that OK. Well, I worded it how I feel, anyway. For such a confident person, Gordon is very slow at making moves. He kisses me every time he picks me up and drops me off. But those kisses don't involve tongues, and they have gone from feeling magical to feeling almost parental. I know I am hardly the world's most sexual person, but I think we should be progressing slightly in our relationship. He should at least come inside my front door.

'But I need to get this written, Flo. God might be able to help me in most things, but he can't do my work for me, can he?'

'I suppose not.'

He pushes his tape back in and carries on singing. When we get to my house, he gives me my usual kiss and says goodnight. I press eject.

'Well, what about Saturday night?' I ask him. 'My mum will be out and I'm babysitting my little sister. Why don't you come over? We can order pizza, watch a movie?'

He looks really unsure.

'Gordon,' I carry on. 'It's normal for two people who like each other to spend a Saturday night in watching a movie, you know,' I say, getting slightly impatient.

'I guess it is. Well, um, OK, I suppose it can't do any harm, can it?'

'No, Gordon, it can't do any harm, so will you come? Eight o'clock?'

'Yes. Yes, OK. I will bring us something to watch. I think I know what you will like.'

'Great.'

'Lovely.'

'Goodnight, Gordon.'

'Goodnight, Flo.'

He puts the tape back in and drives off, singing his songs.

Renée

'Jesus, I want you so bad,' says Dean, throwing me up against his front door. It's midnight, and we have been in the pub. I fancy him so much I have barely been able to keep my hands off him all night.

He opens the door behind me and lifts me into the kitchen, putting me down onto the worktop. He kisses me and pushes a hand up my top. I'm in heaven, but then I nearly pull the toaster out of the socket when the light snaps on and Meg says, 'Oh, sorry, guys. I thought you would be home later. I just had a few hours' kip in your bed, but I can move over to the couch.'

I pull my skirt down and jump off the counter.

'Do you ever go home?' I find myself saying out loud for the first time since this relationship began.

'Excuse me, Renée, whose house is this?' Dean says firmly. Making me feel like a dick.

Meg doesn't answer.

It's obvious I am outnumbered in my belief that Dean and I should get at least one night in this flat without Meg sleeping on the sofa, but she is always here. It's not like she is a housemate – there is no spare bedroom. She just sleeps on the sofa under a thin blanket. Almost every night that I stay over they get really stoned and it's hard to get a conversation out of either of them the more off their faces they get. So I just go to bed and leave them to it. Then Dean and I have sex in the mornings. It's great sex, fun, exciting, proper grown-up sex. I don't use a condom like Dr Burrington told me to, but Dean and I have been seeing each other for over a month now. He hasn't said it yet, but it feels like he is my boyfriend. This is definitely my most serious relationship ever. And with that in mind, I want to 'make love' to my boyfriend before I go to sleep, just once, without thinking Meg can hear every single noise I make.

'Come with me,' I tell him, as I lead him back outside. 'Let's go to my car.' If I can't be alone with him here, I will take him somewhere else.

I'm parked on the pier because all the spaces outside his house were gone when I arrived earlier. I lead him by the hand down the hill. 'I want you to myself tonight,' I tell him. He seems excited.

We get into my car and I put on the engine to get some heat. I roll my driver's seat back and tell him that if he does the same, my car is so small it almost makes a mattress. Flo and I do it all the time. Well, we did until we both got boyfriends.

I take my top straight off. The glow of the lit-up town gives just the right amount of light to make my skin look nice. It's a relief to be topless in front of him without the harsh light of the morning due to his lack of good curtains. I have become very brave with being naked around him, but there is no comparison to how confident I feel when I am not worrying about the marks on my skin.

Having sex in a Fiat 126 isn't easy, but we manage it. And to be honest, apart from the fact that anyone could walk past at any given moment, I am just relieved to get the chance to feel like our sex life is about us, and not just him and his flat, and Meg.

When we are done, we sit in our seats smoking fags. Dean opens a window to try to de-mist the glass. I notice a footprint on the windscreen and we giggle as it disappears when the air comes into the car.

'You seemed to know what you were doing there,' he says, after taking a long drag.

139

'Well, you have taught me a lot in the last month. I know what you like.'

'No, I mean with the car. You had your system down. I take it you've had sex in cars before?'

I wasn't expecting this question. Does it matter? Have I ever asked him about the sex he has had in the bed that I have slept in over ten times now? Why has he even asked me that?

'I'm not sure that's any of your business really, is it?' I say, trying to sound jokey.

'Not my business? Come on, Renée, I don't judge. I am an artist. People express themselves through other people. I like it. I've had girlfriends all over the world. Had sex in cars, on beaches, I've even done it in a cinema. You can tell me about your experiences, can't you? How many people have you slept with?'

I am an open person. Apart from being terrified of buying tampons, not much makes me feel uncomfortable, but this question feels like the most personal thing I have ever been asked. Like telling him would be sharing my biggest secret. No one, not even Flo, knows how many people I have slept with. I find it hard to tell her as her brother is obviously one of the people on the list and we do everything we can to avoid mentioning that. So even though I have told her things I have done with guys, I've never told her how many. But if Dean is going to be my boyfriend and we are going to be honest with each other, then maybe the grown-up thing to do is to tell him the truth.

'Three,' I tell him. 'Including you.'

Well, nearly the truth. He was my fourth.

'Oh come on, you are way too experienced for it to just be three.'

'No, I mean . . . I have been to bed with and done other stuff with more guys. I presume by sleeping with you mean sex? Well, I have had sex with three guys, and yes, one of those was in a car.'

'This car?'

'No, his car.'

'When?'

'Two years ago.'

'Was that your first time?'

'Yes.'

'So you lost your virginity at fifteen? Wow, that's young.'

'Well, I didn't plan it. It just kind of happened.'

'I'm sure it did. You sexy minx, I bet you were gagging for it.'

I start to feel really trapped by my honesty.

'No, I wasn't gagging for it. It's actually not something I am particularly proud of, so can we not talk about it?'

'Sure, I am happy to not talk about it. But four people and you only just turned eighteen? You're racking them up!'

Dean is making me feel bad. Is it really that many? It's barely two a year – is that so bad? It's not like I always have sex the first time I kiss someone, like I did with him. I just went with that because he is so much older than me, I didn't want to appear young. I wanted to behave like the other people he has probably slept with. I wanted to be a woman.

'Well, how many have you slept with then?' I ask, hoping to balance this out.

'More than that, but it's different. I'm older than you.'

'How many had you slept with when you were my age then?'

'More than you. Much more, but it's different, I am a guy.'

'How is it different?'

'Because men fuck and women get fucked, babe. That's why. Women can't behave like men when it comes to sex. It's just the way it is. Come on, let's go back to mine. I fancy a spliff.'

He might as well have called me a slag and been done with it. I don't know what to do with myself.

'I'll drive up,' I say. 'The booze has worn off now, and I saw a space.'

He puts up a little bit of resistance to me driving but it's only up the hill, and he wants to get home. We don't speak again until we pull up outside his house, where I tell him I think I should spend the night at home tonight.

'But what about the morning? I love our mornings,' he says, trying to persuade me with a hand on my thigh and his nose in my neck.

'I'd better get home.'

We kiss and he gets out. I watch him walk in. Meg appears at the kitchen window to wave goodbye to me. I don't wave back.

I drive slowly, knowing that I am way over the limit and that I should not be in my car. As I get to the top of the Grange I think I should have just stayed at Dean's and left early tomorrow morning, but what he said really upset me. 'Men fuck and women get fucked.' What a horrible way to put it. It made sex sound so brutal, so one-sided. All those times we have had sex was he just fucking me? What happened to making love? I am lost in thought and realise that the car has completely steamed up again and a perfect footprint has reappeared on the windscreen. Despite everything, the symbol of my wild, sexy adventures in my car makes me laugh. I swerve slightly out of control and the car crosses onto the other side of the road. I correct myself quickly, and then I see a blue light flashing in my rear-view mirror. Shit, shit shit shit shit shit. I pull over, search my bag for a piece of chewing gum and wind down my window.

'Is this your car?' asks the policeman as he comes up alongside me. He is oldish, with a grey beard. He is shining a torchlight into my face.

'Yes, it's my car.'

'And where have you been so late?'

I am aware that my breath smells of booze, and I am genuinely frightened. I don't want to get caught drink driving. It's so grim. People hate drink drivers, even if they don't kill anyone. It's just a really stupid thing to do. Shit.

'I've been babysitting,' I say, having a stroke of genius. 'The parents didn't get home until really late so I am so tired. I have school tomorrow and my exams start soon. I spent the whole night revising and now I can barely keep my eyes open. I only live around the corner, so I am nearly home.'

I do the best big yawn I can without blowing alcohol breath anywhere near the policeman and wait a very long twenty seconds before he says, 'Well, you must get your sleep if your exams are coming up. That wasn't right of them to stay out so late. Drive safely. I will follow you home to make sure you get back OK.'

When he has walked away I breathe out and pant like I just came up for air. Thank God. But shit, home is actually about another ten minutes away. He will know that I lied, and I am not sure I can drive straight all that way. I do feel really tired.

I have an idea.

Flo

Surely not? I think, as I lie in bed and hear the pebbles being thrown at my window. My heart does a leap. Gordon?

I rush to my window like Juliet rushing to the balcony. Did she even rush to the balcony? I can't remember. Anyway, I tear across my bedroom ready to embrace my love's romantic gesture with open arms. The idea of such romance is overwhelming for me. I have never had a guy come to my house, let alone throw pebbles at my window. It's so, it's so, it's so . . .

It's Renée.

'What are you doing?' I say in a loud shouty whisper out of the window. I see a police car drive past my house slowly, and she turns to give them a wave. What on earth is going on?

'I need to stay here tonight,' she shouts up. 'Let me in!'

Fifteen minutes later, with cups of tea and pyjamas on, Renée and I sit head to toe in my single bed.

'We haven't done this in weeks,' she says.

'It's because we have boyfriends,' I tell her.

'It changes everything, doesn't it?'

'It really does.'

We think about that for a moment. We used to do this all the time, sit in bed for hours and hours drinking tea and talking. Now I don't know what we have to talk about. We are so different all of a sudden.

'So how is *Gordon*?' she asks, a silly smirk on her face.

'He's good. We get on really well, I like him a lot. How's Dean?'

'Yeah, Dean's great. Such a laugh, and it's getting quite serious. Really good. So nice, I'm really happy. Really, really happy.'

'Great.'

'Great.'

We drink some tea and pretend that things don't feel awkward. I'm sure it's just because we haven't seen each other in ages that's making things feel weird.

'Have you been doing any revision?' I ask her, thinking that might warm us up a bit.

'No, but it's OK. I will do some last-minute cramming.'

'The exams start in two weeks, Renée. You'll fail everything again if you don't –'

'All right, Flo, don't go on. What are you, my mum?'

'Jesus, I was just saying,' I say, shocked by how snappy she is being in *my* bed.

'Jesus? I thought that was blasphemy?' she says, like a smart arse.

'OK, so you've still got issues with me believing in God, Renée. I know you think it's a fad, but it isn't, OK?'

'It's just a distraction from the actual stuff that's going on in your life, Flo. It doesn't make you stronger than being the kind of person who deals with stuff properly, like you used to be, does it?'

But that's the thing, I think. I didn't used to deal with stuff properly. I used to hate myself, I used to think everyone hated me. Since going to church I feel far more solid, far more secure. How can that be a bad thing?

'Let's go to sleep,' I say, turning off the light. She is just in a terrible mood. Hopefully by tomorrow she will have calmed down.

In the morning Renée drives us to school. She obviously hasn't come to terms with my choices at all.

'I just don't see where it's all come from,' she says suddenly.

'I know, you've made that very clear.'

'What about other people at school? Do they know you are part of the church now?' I hate the way she says 'part of the church'. It makes it sound so culty. But I think that's how she sees it, as a cult.

'In the book I am reading for English, *Oranges Are Not the Only Fruit*,' Renée goes on, 'the main girl's mum is a crazy religious woman who makes her study the Bible and won't let her read books. And the church is like this horrid institution that people like the mum get obsessive about and judge people who are not in it. And they don't like sex and they don't like freedom, basically. And I thought that was what we are all about at the moment, freedom? And how we are about to break free from school and live our lives in a way we haven't been able to yet. And just as we are about to do that you join the church, which is more controlling than school ever was, even Tudor Falls.'

'Firstly, Renée,' I say, 'the church is nothing like the way it is described in that book you are reading. That's a really extreme example of it. And as far as us being free goes, we will be. If we get into Nottingham then we will have so much freedom. I can do History, you can do English and we will be really happy, like we said.'

'Like *you* said, you mean?'

'No, like *we* said. We made a plan, to go together.'

'No we didn't, Flo, *you* made that plan. Will you stop planning my bloody life for me? You were the one who said I should apply to the polytechnic at Nottingham, not me. I never sent my form, so no matter what happens with my results I am not going to Nottingham, or Bristol, or wherever your third choice was. Jesus, if you took any notice of who I really am you would stop making me feel like shit for not wanting to do what you want me to do.'

'You didn't send off your UCAS form? But you said you were going to the post office,' I say, shocked.

'I know. I did go to the post office. But I threw mine in the bin and sent yours. I don't want to go.'

'So you've been lying to me for the last few months? Making me think we were going together when you never had any plans to come with me at all?'

'Yup.'

My face goes red, but not with embarrassment.

'FUCK YOU FUCK YOU FUCK YOU FUCK YOU!' I scream in her ear as she drives along.

'Flo, chill out! I'll crash!'

'No, Renée, I won't chill out!' I yell. 'It's always something, isn't it? You always have to let me down, or lie, or get whatever you want from a situation and not think about me somehow, don't you?'

'Well, you forced me into this,' she says, swerving the car as she leans away from me. 'This was your plan, not mine. We are different, Flo, bloody hell. You can't make me do something I don't want to do.'

'Stop the car, I want to walk.'

Renée stops slowly, having to use her gears to slow down.

'Maybe we're just too different to be friends, Renée. Maybe it would be easier if we were just honest about that, rather than pretending we can be friends and giving ourselves that stress when we go away. Maybe we should just call it quits now.'

'Fine,' she says, not even looking at me.

'Fine,' I say, slamming the door of her car.

She drives off, and I walk to school. I'm too angry to cry.

6

Bumper to Bumper

Renée

It's our last ever English lesson. That's it now until the exams. This is the moment I have been waiting for. The end of school is so close. I don't have to get up in the morning as my first exam isn't for ten days. I am free, but I don't feel it. I feel more trapped than ever. I haven't spoken to Flo in nearly a week, and I don't want to. I don't want her telling me who I should be – but it's strange. In two years we have hardly ever gone more than a morning without contact. Is that really it? Is our friendship actually over?

I watch Meg from across the room. What *is she* all about? I used to think she was so cool, so chilled out and interesting. Now I realise she's just a tag-along. A drifter. Dean always brushes it off when I ask him why she is always there, why she sleeps under that little blanket on the uncomfortable couch in his flat. But then I guess by the time Meg goes to sleep every night she is so stoned she doesn't notice small details like that.

It does explain how she is so well read, though. I rarely see her at his place without a book in her hands. 'Weed makes me me absorb more,' she tells me often. She says that she 'inhales books' when she is stoned, and that schoolwork is way easier when she has had a few spliffs. I still haven't managed to have more than three drags without passing out myself, so I don't really know what she is talking about.

But the weirdest thing about Meg is the way she is with Dean. What is that relationship all about? She stays there all the time and is completely unfazed by my arrival into the equation, and he just acts like it's completely normal to have an eighteen-year-old girl living in his place. She is always really nice to me. Really non-judgemental about the fact I slept with Dean so quickly. She makes me tea when I go round, she is as lovely to me at school as she ever was, she doesn't seem to be jealous of my relationship with him and she certainly doesn't seem to have a problem with me being there. I can't work it out. Maybe it's me that needs to chill out, but it's so weird. When I ask Dean about it he says, 'She isn't a pain to have around.' So I just have to accept it as part of the deal. There is me, there is Dean and there is Meg. It's bizarre how you can think someone is the coolest person ever, then you get a glimpse of their reality and realise they are actually quite tragic.

And what does it say about Dean? I'm not ready to think too much about that right now, though. I've got enough in my head as it is.

'Have you all checked the timetables? The exam dates are up,' says Mr Frankel. 'Your first English exam is May 23rd. We can meet and discuss the texts if you want to, but otherwise, this is where I leave you. Any questions?'

'Yeah, I've got a question,' says Maggie, rough as ever. 'Where's Emma?'

We all look up from our books and look around the room, even though we know she isn't there. It was the question we have all been wanting to ask for the past two weeks. Mr Frankel looks uncomfortable.

'Emma won't be coming back for the exams,' he says.

'What? Why? She didn't cark it, did she?' barks Maggie, meaning to sound sympathetic but not managing it.

'No, she didn't "cark it", Maggie. She just needs to be somewhere that people can take proper care of her. We are working on a way for her to take the exams at home. It's no secret that she isn't very well.'

I feel happy about this. Happy that Emma is getting the help she needs. Nell should have had that. And I miss Nell these days, I miss her so much I want to run out of the English class and run to Spain to see her. I hope she is all right, that Dad is nice to her. That she is happier than she was with Nana and Pop.

I suddenly realise that this is the moment Aunty Jo was telling me I would have one day. A natural moment where I realise that my sister is one of the most important people in my life. I will call her tonight, and I will make a plan to go and stay with her in Spain this summer. It's the right thing to do.

The bell rings and we all gather our things.

'I'll miss you, Mr Frankel,' I say, not feeling at all silly.

'And me,' says Maggie.

'Me too,' says Martha.

'I will miss you all too,' he says. 'You've been a great class and I know you will all do great in the exams. Hopefully I will bump into you in town one night and you won't have to ignore me, because I won't be your teacher any more.'

We all laugh. I love how unprofessional he is. He's just such a nice man. I do hope our paths cross again – I think he'd probably be really fun to get drunk with.

We leave our English room for the last time.

At home, something is wrong. Aunty Jo is sitting on a bench in the garden, her head down. A shovel is next to her, with blood on it. Oh my God.

'Aunty Jo, what happened? Is it Nana?'

'No, no, Renée,' she says quickly. 'It's Clara. She was killed by a dog this morning. It ran into the garden and straight over to them. Before I could do anything it had poor Clara by the neck. Freddie is heartbroken – look.'

I look over into the area where the geese live and see Freddie, sitting still as anything, his beak down, in a way I have never seen him before. He was always so tall, so proud to protect Clara.

'He looks so sad.'

'There is a breeder up the road who says he has a female, but the deal would be I would have to take two. I was thinking about getting some more pets, so I guess having three geese would be all right. I'm sure you've got revision to do, but you couldn't come with me to pick them up, could you? I think Freddie needs some new love in his life, and quickly.'

'Of course,' I say, happy to do whatever I can to get Freddie back to his usual self.

'It would help me out enormously if you did take the two,' says the man with the geese. 'I have another lot that have just hatched and I need to shift these ones or it's going to be a very overcrowded garden.'

'Yes, that's OK,' says Aunty Jo. 'I am sure Freddie will be delighted with two new girlfriends.'

After a lot of squawking and flapping we manage to get the two female geese into the back of Aunty Jo's car. 'I'll be scraping shit off those seats for the rest of my life now,' she says, laughing at the squelchy splat sounds that keep coming from the back seats. 'Freddie had better appreciate this.'

Carrying a bird each, we head back to the goose enclosure at the end of the garden. Freddie hasn't moved.

'That's the exact spot I found her,' Aunty Jo tells me. 'He hasn't moved from it once. He even has her blood on his feet.'

'It's so sad,' I say. 'Poor Freddie. Do you think we can just replace her? Can the love of your life really just be replaced by someone else?'

'I hope so, Renée. Or Freddie and I are doomed!'

We gently put the birds down inside the gate. They spread their wings and shake their heads, rearranging their feathers to how they looked before Aunty Jo and I messed them up. They eat some of the soggy bread that Freddie hasn't quite managed today and start to explore their new home. Freddie pushes himself up to his feet.

'There you go,' says Aunty Jo. 'Now he sees he has two new

153

lovely ladies to play with. That should cheer him up.'

But Freddie doesn't walk towards Feather and Flapper – the names that came naturally to us to call them – instead he clumps slowly in the opposite direction, his head never reaching up, his beak almost scraping the ground as he walks. He plods around the side of the little house he goes into at night and right around the back and out of sight.

'Let's give him some time to get used to them,' Aunty Jo says. 'I'm sure he'll be fine tomorrow.'

As we walk back up to the house, the impulse to speak to my sister is as strong as it was earlier.

'Is it OK if I call Nell?' I ask Aunty Jo, thinking I already know the answer.

'Oh yes!' she says. 'Use the phone in my room and stay on it as long as you can. Give her my love!'

'I will,' I say, running up to the house. 'I will.'

Flo

Come on, Mum, time to go. Now.

It's seven thirty and my mum is faffing about before she goes on her date. I get her coat and try to put it on her myself. 'Go, you will be late.'

'Flo? What is wrong with you?' says Mum, wrestling with the coat sleeves, finally getting it on. 'I won't be late –'

'Mum?' I tell her, opening the front door. 'Go and have fun.'

The door slams behind her and the smell of cheap perfume is left lingering in the hall. I hope it doesn't put Arthur off her.

I like him. She's been about fifty per cent less hard work since he's been on the scene.

With Abi all tucked up in bed nice and early, it's time to get ready for Gordon. Tonight is the night. I want to move on to the next level of our relationship. Well, maybe just past that actually, as the next stage would literally be just kissing with tongues. But I think I want more than that with him – I am ready. I want us to be a proper boyfriend and girlfriend. At the very least I would like to kiss him properly. Renée was right about one thing – it is normal for people to be sexual.

I run into my bedroom and put on a little bit of blusher and some lip balm. I brush my hair and take it out of the scrunchie it's pulled into, and I spray some deodorant under my arms.

Next, I order some pizza. I thought it might be quite cool to have already ordered pizza so that it arrives shortly after he does. I presume he likes manly-type pizzas, being a man and everything. Renée eats like a man and she always orders the spicy meat feast, so I got him one of those and a ham and pineapple for me. I wonder what she is doing tonight, but then I get the thought of her out of my head. I have to get used to not thinking about her.

I have Cokes in the fridge, and also beers if Gordon and I feel like drinking. During my lunch hour today I ran down to Blockbusters and rented *Dirty Dancing*. It's perfect, because it's a really beautiful love story, but there is a sex scene that I think is the perfect level of sexy for tonight. The main character, Baby, loses her virginity to Johnny, played by Patrick Swayze. It's her first time, but it seems to go really well. It's how I hope my first time goes. It's also a really good one to watch with Gordon as it isn't too explicit, so won't make us feel silly watching it together. Hopefully it will just get us in the mood to do whatever it is we end up doing. If I do think it's going to be awkward, I can just go and make us a cup of tea when the sex scene is coming up. I've seen the movie four times so I know exactly when to leave the room, should I need to. I am terrified but also really excited. This is what boyfriends and girlfriends do, this is normal, this is what should have happened weeks ago. My mouth feels so dry. I also feel a bit sick. The door bell rings.

'Hello, Flo,' Gordon says formally as he passes me a bottle of ginger beer and kisses me on the cheek.

'Hello, Gordon, come in. Can I take your coat?'

'Er . . . thanks,' he says awkwardly. But instead of letting me take it, he shrugs out of it and keeps it bunched up under one arm.

'OK.' Odd, but OK. I start to show him around.

'This is the living room, this is the kitchen, this is the downstairs toilet and up here is my –'

'We don't need to go upstairs,' he says, quickly. 'It's nice down here.'

'Yeah. Of course,' I say, suggesting we go into the living room. I sit on the sofa, he sits on the armchair. 'I ordered pizza and got some movies. I presumed you'd like the spicy meaty one so I got you one of those, and *Dirty Dancing* to watch. It's a love story.'

'Oh, sorry Flo, I'm a vegetarian. And as a matter of fact, I brought a film with me. *Chariots of Fire*. Have you seen it? It's a classic, a must-see for people like us.' He holds out a VHS of the film.

'People like us?'

'People of God.'

Christ!

'I'll just change the order,' I say, gutted that I got it wrong. I run into the hall and call back the pizza place. I catch it just in time.

'I was thinking that maybe, before the movie and the pizza, we could get to know each other a bit,' I say as I go back into the living room, feeling proud of myself for taking control. 'We've spent so much time with other people, and talking about God and the Bible, that I really don't know very much about you. I didn't even know you were a vegetarian. What else should I know about you?' I say, sitting by his feet.

He puts his hand on my head, *his hand on my head*, and says, 'My life is dedicated to Christ. He died for us and I will spend my entire existence on this earth expressing my gratitude for his sacrifice. What else would you like to know, Flo?'

This is hard work. Jesus is like a drug to him. Even in the small amount of time I have known Gordon he has become more and more obsessed. Surely I can distract him from God, for just one night?

'Well, I'd quite like to know the other things about you, not just the stuff related to your faith.'

'Everything about me is related to my faith,' he interjects. 'My life is dedicated to my faith.'

I need to word this differently.

'Yes, but there are other things you like. I mean, do you like sport? If you are a vegetarian, what's your favourite vegetable?'

Did I seriously just ask him what his favourite vegetable is? If we get from cauliflower to kissing over the course of the next three hours it'll be a miracle. Come on, God, I know you are on both of our sides. Help me out with this one, please?

'Flo, you are being a little strange tonight. Is everything all right?'

Strange? Why strange? I am just being interested in him. It's him that's being strange. His body language is so closed. He seems nervous, so unsure of himself compared to usual. It's a very different Gordon to the one who preaches and sings to all of those people. One-on-one Gordon, outside of the confines of his own car, away from God, is quite a different story. But I still want to kiss him.

I stand up and sit back down on the arm of the chair. He jumps up so fast the chair flips to the side from my weight and I land in a heap on the floor with the chair on top of me. When I look up, he has left the room.

'Gordon?' I say, pushing the chair off me and following him into the kitchen. 'What's the matter?' I don't ask him why he didn't bother to help me up, even though I can't believe he just left me squashed under an armchair. I need to sort this out.

'Sorry, Flo, it's just you are coming on so strong,' he says nervously. 'You seem so . . . so desperate. I haven't seen this side of you before.'

'*Desperate?* How am I desperate?'

'Well. The pizza, the sexy movies, the conversation. It's like you've become obsessed with . . . with sex. The reason I was so attracted to you was that you seemed so, I don't know, not into all that . . . sort of innocent. Unsexual.'

UNSEXUAL??

'Gordon, you say you are my boyfriend, but in six weeks you have never even properly kissed me. We have never walked down a street holding hands. We should be at third base by now – that would be normal.' I'm not really sure what I mean by 'third base'.

'Flo, I believe in chastity before marriage. You need to know that and respect it.'

'You what?'

'I follow the word of the Bible. Sexual purity. No sex until marriage. All of this, this *seduction*, is just so predatory. It isn't about love, or the sanctity of marriage, or the word of our dear Lord Jesus Christ.'

'NO, it isn't to do with any of those things. It's about an eighteen-year-old girl who has never been laid who should at least be allowed to see her boyfriend's penis if she feels like she might be ready to do so!'

Oh my, did that just come out of my mouth? God? Did you make me say that? I didn't even know I was capable of saying something like that.

We stand in total silence for about two whole minutes.

'I think I had better go,' he says.

'I think you should too,' I say crossly, not bothering to walk him to the door.

No sooner do I hear the front door shut than the door bell rings, almost instantly.

Gordon has come back! I run to the door and open it, ready to be ravished.

'Pizza?' says a little man wearing a bike helmet. He's only

159

holding one box.

'I ordered two pizzas.'

'Your friend took his.'

'Great,' I say, handing over some money. 'That's just great.'

Renée

'Do you believe in God?' I ask Dean as he lies next to me in bed reading *Trainspotting*. It's our usual Sunday-morning routine. I have been plucking my eyebrows in my hand mirror for a while. Is it just me or do eyebrows grow more when you've been drinking?

'I'm spiritual,' he says. 'I got quite interested in Buddhism when I was in Thailand, but Christianity is bullshit to me. Just a way to make humans feel guilty for being human.' He carries on reading.

I dig away at a short hair above my left eye that is starting to drive me a bit mad.

'I just don't get it,' I say. 'Why people have to focus on a story. It's just a book of children's stories. Imagine if a guy turned up on Guernsey now and started saying he was the son of God. We would all think he was mad. I think Jesus was just a madman who was really convincing. He gave people something they needed to hear, an explanation of our existence, but he made it up. He was just a loony who was talking bollocks. But he was probably really handsome, so everyone just fell for it. They still fall for it.'

He lowers his book. 'OK, what brought this on?'

'It's my closest friend, Flo. She's turned to God. She lost her dad a few years ago and I think it's about that, but it's freaking me out.'

He puts his book on his belly. 'Flo? You haven't mentioned her before. Who is she then?'

'She's my best friend. At least she was. Have I really never mentioned her?'

And it strikes me – Dean knows nothing at all about me. It's been six weeks and he has never asked me anything about me but I know so much about him. I read his work, I know who his friends are, where he grew up, where he has travelled to. He has even told me in tiny detail about some of the women he has slept with. I acted interested even though I didn't really want to hear it, but when I tried to tell him about my past he just dismissed it like it was unimportant, because 'that kind of sex was meaningless', and that making love to him for the first time was when I really started to understand how a man and a woman are supposed to connect sexually. It isn't that I disagree with that entirely, but I don't like brushing off my past as 'meaningless'. It all meant something to me at the time.

We have sex a lot, much more than we talk. He is a bit obsessed with sex. Everything turns him on. He wants it all the time, and I find it quite hard to keep up, if I'm honest. I used to get really horny and crave sex, but now I barely get the chance. He decides he wants it, and before I have got in the mood, we do it. I miss working up to it in my own time. I rarely get the chance to instigate sex any more, because he always gets in there first, and that means a lot of the fun for me has gone. But I guess this is just what having a proper sexual relationship is like. It's more functional. And there is a lot more sex than chat.

Dean and I hardly chat at all.

We go to the pub, but Meg is usually there, and when she isn't Dean usually just tells me about ideas for plays that he has, and articles he needs to write for the *Globe*, and how he is waiting for the 'perfect story' to break him into the real world of journalism. Then after the pub we come back to his. He and Meg stay up and get stoned, I go to bed, and in the morning we have sex, then some more sex, and then he reads and I usually leave. And I feel horrid when I leave, because ever since he said that thing, 'Men fuck, women get fucked', sex feels so one-sided. Not to mention how he made me feel about the amount of people I've slept with. There is a shadow over me now, a feeling of guilt about the way I have behaved before. I was always so confident sexually, and now I feel so self-conscious about it all. And that seems unfair, seeing as he is quite open about the fact that he has shagged his way around the world. I worry he has ruined sex for me now. I can't get his words out of my head while we do it – he's taken the fun out of it.

The routine of spending Sunday mornings with him, then not having any contact until around Tuesday, then him calling me and asking me over so we can do it all again is such an odd thing to do with a person who knows nothing about me. I have mentioned Aunty Jo numerous times, but he has never asked me why I live with her, or if I have sisters or brothers, or where my mum is, or my dad. So maybe this is my moment, this is the next step of our relationship. This is the moment

162

I can tell him a bit about who I am. Maybe if he knew more about me, the sensitivity would come back to the sex. Maybe he would care about me more.

'I've never really told you anything about me, have I?' I say, starting slowly. Trying not to sound upset that he has never asked me anything.

'No, but I have worked out what you like, haven't I?' he says, running his hand up my inner thigh.

'No, not just sexually. I mean about me, my life. Don't you want to know a bit more about me? I mean, you don't know anything.'

'OK, if you need to tell me stuff, tell me.' He lies back flat and moves his book to the floor.

'OK, well. I used to live with my nana and Pop with my mum and my sister, but my mum died of breast cancer when I was seven.'

He doesn't react, though I thought he would say something. I carry on.

'After she died my sister Nell and I carried on living with our grandparents. Oh, I forgot to say that my mum and dad split up when she got ill. My grandpa basically made him leave. He lives in Spain now and has a new wife and two other children. Nell got really anorexic a couple of years ago and ended up in hospital. All she really wanted was to be with Dad, so when Aunty Jo, my mum's sister, came back to Guernsey after her divorce she called Dad, because my grandpa hated him, and arranged for Nell to go out and be with him. And now Nell lives there. We never really got on and haven't spoken much over the last few years, but recently I've been missing her, and we spoke on the phone the other night and it was actually really nice. I think I might go to Spain for a few weeks this summer after the exams. But it will be scary, because I don't have a relationship with my dad. When I talk to him it's awkward and I just don't feel like he knows me. But it's OK because I live with Aunty Jo now and Nana lives with us too. Pop died last year. Nana has dementia and is getting madder by the day. Dean? Are you listening?'

He is so still I wonder if he has fallen asleep. But his eyes are open, so he is awake. Good, I didn't want to have to say all that again.

'Christ, it's all a bit depressing, isn't it?' he says, sighing. 'It's bringing me down. Do we have to do this on a Sunday morning?'

Bringing him down? What a cruel thing to say. If he feels brought down hearing it, how does he think I felt living it? And what has it being Sunday morning got to do with anything? Am I supposed to choose when I offer him nuggets of real-life information to fit in around his down time? I hoped he might commend me on how together I am after experiencing all of that stuff. Which, I have to admit, sounds pretty horrific when explained in one go.

'Yeah, I guess so, but I am not depressed about it. It's just the way my life has been and I –'

He cuts me off. 'Well, I guess it explains a few things.'

'What do you mean?'

'Well, why you've put yourself around a bit. Must be about the attention, I suppose.'

I have to stop myself from panting like a dog. It feels like

164

he stabbed me in the lung.

'What is that supposed to mean?' I manage to get out.

'I mean, it's pretty textbook behaviour for a girl who wasn't loved by her daddy. Literature is full of those characters.'

'Did you listen to anything I just told you?' I ask him, wondering if he heard the bit about how I lost my mum, how my sister nearly killed herself, how I live with my aunty now. I told him so many things and the only one he thought to mention was my sex life?

'Oh come on, don't get upset. I'm just saying that for a girl of your age to have slept with all of those people, there had to be an underlying reason.'

'What about all the people you have slept with? What is your "underlying reason"?'

'Babe, I told you. I am a guy, it's just different.' He tries to pull me towards him. 'Come on, what you need is some sex to take your mind off all that stuff.'

'Why would you want to have sex with someone like me?' I ask, meaning it, if he thinks so lowly of me.

'Because I like girls who are a bit fucked up.'

I know that I will regret forever not telling him that he is the fucked-up one, not me. But I don't seem to have the confidence to say it.

He runs his hands over my body. I feel lost as to what to do. How can someone who makes me feel so guilty for being sexual then want me to be so sexual?

We have sex. I hate myself for it. I have never felt so self-conscious. To be enthusiastic makes me feel like a slut, to be unresponsive makes me look hurt, and I don't want him to think I am hurt. I also don't want him to think I am a slut.

Why, after I told him all of those things about my life, did he think sex was what I needed today? What I really needed was acknowledgement, a conversation.

It dawns on me then. Dean doesn't care about me at all.

Flo

Clearing out my locker in the common room for the last time, I feel like crap. Why did I have to pick a bigger virgin than me to be my first boyfriend? Even though I know Gordon not wanting to go further with me isn't really about me, the rejection is still making me feel horrible. I believe in God too, but I do want to live a normal life. I want a boyfriend who fancies me, I don't want to wait until I get married to lose my virginity. I find myself thinking about sex more than ever, it's all around me at the grammar, with the boys here too. I feel like I want to know now – I want to have it. I think. Oh maybe I don't . . . I would probably be crap at it anyway – my coordination is awful.

There are plenty of people I know who have sex and who go to church. You don't have to abstain the way Gordon does. Look at Madonna. She has sex all the time and never shuts up about God. How come she's allowed? Are there two Bibles?

Having a relationship with someone like Gordon would be impossible. There would be three people present at all times. Him, me and *Him*. I don't think I want to be with someone who can't put me first. I'm probably better off without him.

166

'Kerry!' I shout as I see her come in on the other side of the room.

I go over to her, but she doesn't smile. She glares at me in fact. I just don't get it. What's her problem?

After a couple of minutes of really awkward silence I decide to clear the air.

'Kerry, I thought we were friends, but for weeks you have acted like you regret inviting me into the group. Did I do something to offend you?'

'I don't know what you're talking about,' she says blandly, but then she clocks the expression on my face and looks softer, like she's realising she is being unfair.

'Oh Flo,' she says, shrugging. 'You didn't do anything. It's me, not you.'

'What do you mean?' I ask, confused.

'I'm –'

She is cut off by the sound of Bernadette's voice, who has crept up on us and cornered us at the back of the common room.

'What's up with you two? Arguing about which disciple you are most like? You look like a Peter, Kerry. Yeah, definitely a Peter. And Flo Parrot? Are you a God-loving virgin too now? Well, you definitely look like a Paul, with your big nose.'

Bernadette finds this hilarious and she and her two ugly friends start laughing and one of them says, 'You crack me up, B. So funny.'

'Just ignore her,' says Kerry. 'She will go away.'

'What is her problem with you?' I ask, but before Kerry has the chance to answer Bernadette is up close in our faces and obviously has more to say.

'Jesus can't help you with being a little lezzer, can he, Kerry?'

'You can't call her that,' I say, wanting to stick up for my friend.

'Oh, hasn't she told you? She's a dirty little lezzer. And don't go telling me you're not her girlfriend. You look like a lezzer too, with your weird clothes.'

Bernadette is now right up in my face. She is so mean. I want to fight back to her, stick up for me and Kerry, but I can't. She catapults me back to the old me, who let Sally put me down. I feel incapable of self-defence and do nothing to stop her saying what she wants to say. I'm still as pathetic as I ever was.

'Dirty little lezzers, both of you.'

We all jump as the door of the common room swings open. Renée bursts in. It couldn't be more obvious what is happening. I feel instantly relieved. Bullies like Bernadette are nothing to her. She is here to stick up for her best friend.

Or maybe not.

Renée takes in what is going on, looks me right in the eye, then turns around and leaves.

It's all the confirmation I need. Our friendship really is over.

'Go on, lez off,' instructs Bernadette, forcing us out of the common room. She shouts, 'Lezzers!' after us one more time, just for fun. We leave to the sound of her cackles.

'You never told me you were a lesbian,' I say to Kerry as we walk across the car park, realising that I have never, to my knowledge, met a lesbian.

'It's not something I shout about.'

'So what's Bernadette's problem with you? How does she know?'

'I guess you could say, she's my ex.'

Wow. I was not expecting that.

'She used to come to our church. We were best friends. Then it turned into something else, something deeper. Bernadette was never at ease with it though, never able to admit who she really was. Then one day her mum caught us in Bernadette's bedroom together and she made Bernadette stop coming to the group, and the entire family started going to another church. Ever since then Bernadette has been vile to me. It's just an act, she knows that I know the truth about her. But she is full of so much fear that she has to live her life being someone else. I feel sorry for her in some ways.'

I try really hard not to react too strongly to what Kerry is telling me. Instead I turn the conversation back to us. I'll process the other stuff later.

'And what about me? Why have you been so off with me?'

We stop by my car.

'I like you, Flo. I've watched you in RS all year. When you helped me that day I thought you felt the same. You seemed to go out of your way. Then you started going out with Gordon and I didn't know what you were playing at.'

'Wait, you thought I was gay?'

'I guess we all get it wrong sometimes.'

'Why? Why did you think I was gay?' I feel bad for making this about me, but I am really insulted and need her to clarify.

'The way you dress, the way you were with Renée. I just presumed you were in love with her but that she didn't feel the same way, so if I stepped in you would want to be with me instead.'

How is it possible to feel so offended, but at the same time so happy that one person on this earth finds me desirable?

'Well, I'm not a lesbian, and I'm not in love with Renée. I wasn't then and I certainly am not now. Not after what she just did.'

'You can't blame her for not coming over. Bernadette isn't exactly inviting,' says Kerry, not quite getting what happened.

'No, you don't understand. Renée isn't ever afraid of people like her. She didn't come over because our friendship is over. She doesn't care any more.'

Suddenly, explosive tears come out of me. The realisation that I have lost Renée, that boys don't fancy me and that girls think I am a lesbian is all too much.

'I'm going to go home,' I tell Kerry. 'I'm sorry you thought I was gay. I'm not.'

'I'm sorry I've been off with you,' says Kerry. 'It's not easy being eighteen and the only "out" lesbian in a year of 150 people.'

I am starting to wonder if being eighteen and anything is easy.

Renée

I've done loads of stuff I'm ashamed of, but I think walking away from Flo when she was being bullied might be the worst ever. What kind of person am I? I can go on as much as I like about why I think religion is a load of bullshit, but at least all she is doing is trying to be a better person. What am I doing?

I just couldn't bring myself to go over and stick up for her. I couldn't back Flo up this time, I wouldn't have known what to say. I couldn't think of a single way to stick up for what she believes in. But I feel like total crap and really hate myself right now. I am a shit friend, Dean thinks I'm a slut and I have no idea what I want to do with the rest of my life. Good one, Renée. Good one.

Over in the lay-by it's just me, Pete and Marcus. They're being their usual pervy selves.

'Been getting any lately then, Renée?'

'Oh fuck off, Pete. Is that seriously all you think about?' I snap.

'All right, Period Face, calm down. It was you who told us once that you think about sex eighty-five per cent of the time, so don't get all narky because we believed you.'

Pete's right. I did say that. WHY did I say that? I ask for all the shit that comes my way.

'Cheer up, Renée,' Pete says. 'Let's play chicken. Come on, I want to see that little Fiat of yours racing towards me at – how fast does it go? Ten miles an hour?' They fall into stitches. Apparently the fact that I have a car that comfortably trots along at the Guernsey speed limit of thirty-five miles an hour is hilarious.

'I'm not playing chicken, you idiots. It's such a stupid game,' I say, feeling like I don't really want to do anything but smoke hundreds of cigarettes and mope around being sad about Flo.

'I'll play it,' says a voice behind me. It's Matt Richardson, in his school uniform.

My instinct is to tell him to bugger off, but then I think of Flo, and how I just abandoned her, and that Matt is her friend, and I think maybe, if I make friends with Matt, then that would be a respectful thing to do for Flo. It would make my apology, which she probably won't even want to hear, much easier and more sincere. So I turn to him and hope he isn't one of those religious types who doesn't shut up about Jesus.

'Hi Matt, how are you?' I say.

He looks stunned.

'Me? I'm fine . . . ' He hesitates, presumably stumped for any kind of conversation that doesn't involve Jesus or cars. 'So, shall we play chicken? I drive my uncle's car around his field at the weekends, I can drive a manual fine. If I don't go on the road and we just stick to the car park then we're not breaking the law. Can I?'

'You're not old enough to drive though,' I say. 'And my car doesn't have any brakes.'

Pete sneaks up behind me and whispers in my ear. 'Don't worry, it's all for show. Just make sure he keeps driving straight, I will turn off.'

So there IS a system? It's basically wrestling for cars. It's all planned beforehand.

'Please?' asks Matt again.

Oh God. Chicken really is my worst nightmare. I get so scared when other people are driving, I scream all the time thinking they are too close to the kerb. But I'm still thinking that if I bond with Matt, I might stand a chance of winning back Flo. And that's all that matters.

'OK. But I have to come in the car with you to teach you how to stop.' I throw him the keys.

He drives me around the corner to the big empty car park of the sports field. To be fair, he does know how to drive a car. 'OK, Matt,' I say, 'shall we go to Flo's house after this? We could pick her up? Go have a cup of tea and some chips at the Vazon caff?'

'Sounds great,' he says vaguely, more focused on driving than he is on me. I am happy. This was a good idea. Flo will forgive me, she forgives everybody.

He drives all the way to the end of the car park and turns around. Pete and Marcus are facing us about a hundred feet away.

'Pete *always* turns off, OK? So you just keep going straight, no matter how close they get, just keep going straight. They will think you are really tough and cool if you have the balls to keep going straight, but Pete will turn. I know he will. When they have passed, take your foot off the accelerator and I will talk you through slowing down using the gears. My brakes don't work, OK?

'OK.'

I have a horrible feeling about this. But Pete knows what he is doing, he has done this a thousand times. And as long as Matt keeps driving straight then everything will be fine. Deep breath. I am playing chicken to save my friendship. This is good. I stick my arm out of the window and give a thumbs-up, and Pete does the same. We're off.

'Remember, just keep going straight,' I remind Matt. Then I roll my eyes, this is so stupid. 'Oh, and don't bother putting your foot to the floor straight away. You pick up more speed if you do it slowly. My car has its own rules.'

He does what I say and we start creeping forward. Before long we are at 15mph, which feels fast in a car park. Pete and Marcus are racing much quicker towards us, both their faces like melons with teeth. They're so excited. This, for them, is living. The speed feels frightening now, I don't like it. I want to shut my eyes until they have turned off and Matt has driven past them, but then Matt panics. It's like he doesn't trust the game. His right hand pulls down the steering wheel.

'Matt, NO! What are you doing! They will turn. They *always* turn!'

But he doesn't trust me. He turns sharply to the right at exactly the moment Pete turns to his left. I reach for the steering wheel and try to push it back, but it's too late. He looks at me, I look at him. There's a loud screech. I don't know if it's Matt, or the brakes, or me. Then a slam, so loud it feels like a punch in my head. More screeching, a creak of a door. I feel like I'm under water. The red of Pete's car is too close – is that what is on my hands too? I'm too trapped to move. My head is too heavy and I can't find my voice.

I have to sleep.

7

Say You'll Be There

Flo

'Dear God, I'm lost again. I thought I was working myself out, but I haven't. I have no idea what kind of person I am. Those feelings I had for Gordon weren't real, even though I tried to tell myself they were. As soon as he was out of my life I forgot about him. What are those short bursts of infatuation about? Renée has them all the time with boys. How are you supposed to know which ones to sleep with and which ones not to sleep with? I don't want to sleep with the ones I don't care about a week later, but how do you know that you'll go off them? Sorry, can I talk to you about this stuff? I am feeling like the only person I have is you, which I guess is what I wanted in the first place, but I didn't think I would lose Renée completely. I just don't know what her and I are any more. She doesn't accept me at all. I think she's using the whole university thing as an excuse to get out of our friendship, and it's making me so sad. But I am who I am. I used to think I could change for people, but I'm not so sure I'm easy with that any more. God, please send me a sign that will show me what to do. Do I fight for my friendship, or do I just let her go? I –'

The doorbell rings loudly three times in a row and snaps me out of my moment with God. It's annoying, like being woken from a really deep sleep. But whoever it is seems desperate.

'OK, OK,' I say, walking to the door as they persistently bang on it. 'I'm coming, calm down.'

I open the door. It's Kerry. She's crying. Really crying. I thought we had established that I wasn't gay?

'Flo,' she says, hardly able to get her words out. 'There's been an accident. Matt, he's . . . ' She hiccups and struggles to catch her words.

'It's OK. Breathe, breathe. Matt what?' I push, trying not to presume anything until she has said it.

'He's . . . dead.'

For a moment nothing comes to me. My head goes white, thoughtless, like I've never thought of anything before. Then Kerry falls onto me like a rag doll, and I realise that what I have to do is take care of her.

'Come in. Come on, I will make you some tea. It's OK, you'll be OK. Everything will be OK,' I say like clockwork.

But of course it won't.

I sit her on a chair in the kitchen and put the kettle on. That's what you do, isn't it? When someone is having a nightmare and you need a moment to work out what to say? You put the kettle on. My own shock. My own feelings. They have to

176

be contained. I have to make sure Kerry is all right. Matt has been her friend for years, mine only for a matter of months. I'm sad but I can control it, she needs me to control it. I have to make her tea, and let her cry, and hold back my own tears and tell her that I am here for her and that everything will be OK. Even though it won't be. I make the tea as quickly as I can and pull up a chair to sit next to her.

'Kerry, Kerry,' I say, trying to urge her to stop crying and talk to me. 'Kerry, tell me what happened.'

'Chicken . . . ' she says.

She must be so confused.

'Chicken?'

'He was playing chicken, in the lay-by. They crashed,' she tells me, through her tears.

I can't believe it. Poor Matt. Renée always told me how the boys played chicken and how dangerous it was.

'He was in Renée's car,' she finishes, managing to look me in the eye.

This time my thoughts don't stop; they speed up. I see my best friend smashed up on the bonnet of her car. The horror must show on my face.

'No. Renée is OK, no, no, she's OK,' Kerry says, seeing instantly where my imagination had taken me. I breathe the kind of breath you can only breathe when your entire body wanted to stop forever.

Thank God, thank you, God. Thank you.

'Matt was driving,' she continues, managing to control herself a little better. 'He was killed on impact. Renée has a broken arm, but she's OK.'

Every answer I ever needed comes to me at once. The thought of losing Renée, I mean really losing Renée, nearly killed me on the spot.

'Come on, I'll drive you home.' I help Kerry up. I need to get to Renée as quickly as I can.

Renée

I keep playing it back in slow motion. Up until it all went black. I keep seeing it happen over and over again. How I knew Pete's car was going to hit us before it even did. A split second before, Matt and I looked at each other and I knew then he was going to die. He did too – we knew. I've never seen that fear in someone's face before. There was me so worried about my brakes not working when they couldn't have saved us anyway.

I should never have let him drive my car.

When I came around all I could see was red. My legs, my hands, all red and wet. It took me a few seconds to realise it was blood. When I did, I thought I was dying. I tried to lift my head, but it hurt too much, and my arm too. I couldn't move it. I felt the pressure of something against my left side, like I was wedged against something. I tried to shift my body but it hurt to move, and then I noticed a hand on my leg. It wasn't my hand. And then I realised that the thing pressing against me was Matt. He was limp and heavy. He was squashed against me, because the bonnet of Pete's car was pushing through the driver's door of mine. I knew instantly he was dead. So, so dead. I was covered in blood, and none of it was mine.

'Renée, here, drink this.' Aunty Jo puts a cup of tea onto the kitchen table next to me.

'Where is Nana?' I ask her, worried she can see me.

'Don't worry, she's watching TV in bed. She doesn't know.'

Relieved, I drink some tea.

'Aunty Jo, did I kill someone today? Matt's dead because of me, isn't he?' I cry more. I feel like I will cry forever.

She kneels down and takes my right hand in hers. My left one is hanging pathetically out of the end of a sling.

'You listen to me. Matt chose to drive your car, OK? Those boys wanted to play that game, OK? If he hadn't been in your car he would have done it in someone else's. This is not your fault.'

'OK,' I say, not convinced.

The doorbell rings. Aunty Jo goes to answer it. Two minutes later, Mr Frankel is standing in our kitchen. It's very strange to see him at home, but I'm too wrecked to question it.

'Hello, Renée,' he says.

I can't say anything.

'How's she doing?' I hear him say to Aunty Jo, as they realise I am not capable of being involved in a conversation. Their voices sound like they're under water. The room feels so hot, so clammy.

'Not good, understandably. I don't know what to say to her.'

'The school wanted to send someone over. I have spent more time with her over the last few years than anyone else, as we realised pretty quickly that English was the only class she really came to. I am so fond of Renée. I hope you don't mind the visit?' says Mr Frankel to Aunty Jo.

'Not at all. Thank you for coming. Tea?'

Their pleasantries make me want to scream. I want them to shut up so much. How does anyone think they can make this better? Matt is dead because of me. I shouldn't be alive either.

'I need air,' I say, finding it harder and harder to breathe.

Aunty Jo goes to open a window and Mr Frankel comes over to me and kneels down. I can't handle another person kneeling down telling me I will be OK. Or that it isn't my fault. Neither of those things are true. I need to get out.

'I need the sea,' I blurt as I run for the door. Mr Frankel tries to stop me, but I break free of him and I run, and run, and run, and I will keep running until I get to a place where I can breathe.

Flo

After seeing Kerry into her house I make my way straight over to Renée's. She must be so hurt, so frightened. She is strong, but not for this kind of stuff. Who is? I just want to make sure she is all right. It's a force so powerful in me that even if I wanted to ignore it, I couldn't.

'You don't send messages in halves, do you, God?' I say, looking up.

I feel him more than ever. This is the moment I have been waiting for. The feeling that he is guiding me, that I know who I am, what my purpose is. My purpose is to help my friend, to be the best friend I can be. I pull up at the house and run in through the open front door.

'Renée?' I shout, looking around downstairs. I start to run up to her room, but it's empty. 'Renée?' I shout, coming back down. 'Jo? Oh, Mr Frankel. What are you doing here?'

'I came to check in on Renée.'

'How is she? Where is she?'

'She isn't here. She ran off about an hour ago, saying she needed to be at the sea. Jo went looking for her and I said I would stay here in case she came back.'

'Where's her nana?'

'She's fine, watching TV. She doesn't know anything. I have taken her tea.'

'I will find her,' I say, running back to my car. 'I'll drive around the entire coast of Guernsey until I do.'

'I'll stay here for as long as I have to,' Mr Frankel shouts after me.

Driving past town the moon is so bright that the sky looks dark blue. I have driven along every coast road and screamed her name on every beach and I still haven't found Renée. Maybe she's gone home. I decide to head back. If she isn't there I will come back out. I will drive all night if I have to.

And then it strikes me.

The place that she would go to at a time like this, the place I know makes her think about living life, and dealing with death.

Our wall.

I turn left at Havelet Bay and look along the top of the long wall that goes from the edge of town all the way out to sea. And there I see the silhouette of my broken friend. Sitting on the very spot where I should have known she would be.

A few years ago, when Renée and I first became friends, she brought me here and persuaded me to jump off the wall and into the sea. I hadn't wanted to, but her insistence that we should be fearless, and that taking that plunge would mean we were living our lives to the full, is what eventually made me do it. So I took off my shoes and we jumped in holding hands. She was right, I had never felt so alive as when we crawled out of that cold water, our school uniforms waiting for us on the wall. Then, months later, she brought me here again, this time to throw my dad's ashes into the sea. With Abi in between us, we watched the box containing them drift away from us in the moonlight.

I haven't been back up here since.

'Renée?'

She looks up at me. Her face is so puffy, so sad and bruised.

'Have you come to tell me you hate me?'

'Of course I haven't,' I say, sitting down next to her. Our legs dangle over the edge of the wall. The sea is not very high and quite rough. It doesn't feel very safe.

'I let you down and then killed your friend. How can you not hate me?'

A small knife twists in my stomach as I think of Matt. I try to ignore it for now.

'Nothing that happened before matters, OK?'

'It does, though, doesn't it? Because it all adds up on the list of things that I have done wrong to you. We were going to come and see you, me and Matt. That's why I let him in the car, that's why I said he could play chicken. So that afterwards he would come with me to get you and we would go to Vazon caff and have chips. That was all I wanted.'

'I would have loved that,' I say, putting my arm around her. She shrugs me off because her shoulder is so sore.

'How are you feeling?' I ask, knowing it's a stupid question, but hoping it urges her to talk more. She stares out to sea like something is going to appear on the horizon and help her. I wish she would just look to her right and realise that it's me.

I close my eyes and ask God for the strength to help me do this.

'You can get through this, Renée. It's just going to take a bit of time.'

'What do you know about time? We're eighteen. We think we have lived, but we haven't even started. I thought I had suffered all the pain I had to suffer when my mother died, but life has got harder, not easier. Time means nothing, all it does is give more chance for things to go wrong.' She cries and I can see it hurts. Hurts in the way it does when you have cried so much that your eyes can't make any more tears. I know that feeling. I take her good hand and we sit in silence looking out to sea. I tell myself not to speak until I know what to say.

'Can I pray for you?' is what eventually feels right.

'Oh Flo, why don't you rub it in?'

'Rub it in, how?'

'With God. Good for you, having God. Good for you. I'm glad you have someone up there to talk to that you believe is there. Some of us aren't so lucky. I've talked to Mum every day for the last eleven years and she has never answered me. I don't believe she's anywhere really, I just talk. Talk to the ceiling, talk to the walls, talk to the bath. But I know she can't hear me. I don't have faith and I can't make myself have it. I just picture her and throw words out there, knowing they fall to the ground. Then you just get it, like it's the easiest thing. You just connect with God and make it sound so easy.'

'How do you know she can't hear you?'

'Because when people die, they die. She's nowhere.'

'I used to think that too, but then I realised that heaven makes me happy. That if Dad is there then one day I will see him again. That if I talk to him, he is somewhere, and he can hear me. It's nice.'

She suddenly seems very angry. She stands up.

'Well, if Mum is somewhere, then your dad is there too, and Matt, and Pop, and everyone else who has died. They're somewhere, are they? Waiting for us? Well, let's go and see them.'

She starts to undo her laces with her right hand.

'Renée, what are you doing?'

'I'm going to jump.'

'But you could drown. It's rough, and your arm?'

'If I drown, won't that be the work of God? Maybe he will save me. Maybe not. If he doesn't, I'll see Mum, right? You say she is in heaven? Well, I want to see her.'

I get down onto the path, hoping she will follow me.

'Renée, come down, please. This is silly. Let's go home, get some tea and talk.'

'What's talking going to do? Who is that going to bring back? This is the spot, Flo. It's made us feel alive and it's helped us deal with death. So let's see which one it's to be tonight.'

She launches herself forward and I try to catch her but can't.

The splash of her body hitting the water seems freakishly loud.

God? What are you trying to do?

I kick off my shoes and pull myself back onto the wall. Looking down I can't see her. Where did she go? A bright light flashes from the beach and with that I see her, face down, bobbing and lifeless. Without thinking twice, I tear off my coat and jump in after her.

The water is so cold, and without the adrenaline of excitement it feels dangerous and scary. Breathing is hard, but I'm so focused on finding Renée that I can cope, somehow. The light from the beach is shining directly onto her now, and I can see her bobbing just a few feet from me. I swallow a huge glug of salty water that makes me cough and choke, but I don't stop. I reach her and flip her over. She's breathing but her eyes are closed. Looping my elbow under her chin, I swim to the shore. It feels like a lifetime away but I finally make it. Behind the light I see Aunty Jo. She runs into the sea, picks Renée up and runs with her towards the road. I stay for a second, on all fours, my lungs tight from the cold, the waves lapping at my feet, and I let my tears come.

8

Viva Forever

Renée

Three days have passed since the accident. Flo left me for the first time this morning. She needed to go home to do some revision, but I couldn't give a shit about the exams right now. I don't want to be anywhere but my bedroom. As soon as I leave it, someone asks me how I'm feeling. Such a stupid question.

I wonder if I will ever have an answer other than 'like the weight of a dead person is leaning against my left side'. Because that's the truth. My broken arm is sore and it reminds me of Matt's body, because that's what crushed it. My left arm will always be associated with him now, and that will always be attached to me. So I will never escape this. I'm trying to be grateful that I'm still alive and to remind myself that I'm really lucky, but life has changed forever.

Matt dying is the strangest feeling. I'm not grieving, because

I didn't know him. I can't think back to loving memories or feel sad because I lost a friend, because I didn't. My feelings are so much more disconnected than that. It's about guilt, and regret. I should never have let him drive my car. I knew chicken was a bad idea, but I let my guard down and I was so stupid to do it. And now two people have lost their son and I know that they must be hurting so much. I feel bad that I will walk away from this with a sore arm and a bad memory, but they will never see their son again.

There's a knock on my bedroom door. 'The phone, for you. I think it's Dean,' says Aunty Jo, passing me the phone.

'Hello?' I say.

'Renée, babe, it's me. I hadn't heard from you in a few days, I missed your body. Then Meg told me what happened, I can't believe it. Are you OK?'

I hadn't been able to call him, I didn't know how to explain what happened, but I am so happy to hear that he cares.

'It's horrible, Dean. So horrible.'

'Babe, I can't imagine what you're going through. You must be in such a state. I want to see you, you can tell me everything.'

'Are you home all day?' I ask.

'All day. I won't go out, just come when you can. I'm here for you, babe.'

'Thank you.' I hang up. Aunty Jo comes back in.

'Flo called while you were sleeping. She said she wondered if she should come here so we can all go to the funeral together on Saturday.'

'Sure,' I say, robotically.

'And I was wondering how you were feeling. Maybe this is

the right time to go and see Mr and Mrs Richardson. I know it's terrifying, but I do think it's the right thing to do before the funeral.'

I roll onto my side. It hurts.

'I can't,' I cry. Proving that no amount of crying can dry up the tears of a tragedy like this.

'Yes, you can. Come on.'

Aunty Jo guides me out of bed and into the bathroom.

'Wash your face, clean your teeth, and let's go and do the right thing.'

As we pull up to Matt's house the reality of what happened strikes me again. It's such a lovely house. Big and pretty, an old Guernsey farmhouse with ivy growing up it and a lovely door with a sign saying *Sunset View*. I imagine him walking home from school and his mum opening the door and cuddling him. I know he was really close to her. He went for hot chocolate in town with her – I don't know anyone else who goes for hot chocolate in town with their mum. I've felt nerves before, but this is different. I don't feel like there are butterflies in my tummy, I feel like there are rats scratching around. I have to concentrate hard not to let them run up my throat.

'OK?' says Aunty Jo. 'Are you ready?'

I'm not ready. How can you ever be ready for something like this? They must hate me so much. I bet they wish I was dead, that Matt had the broken arm and that my ribs and lungs were crushed instead.

'Do you want me to come in with you?' Aunty Jo asks.

'What if she tries to hit me?'

188

'She won't try to hit you, but if she is angry and needs to express that, you have to accept it. Coming here is very brave, and I am sure they will appreciate it. You want me to come?'

'No, I'd better do this on my own. You stay here with Nana.'

'You were always the best dancer. You can do it,' says Nana, somehow picking up on my nerves even if she hasn't a clue what's going on.

I get out of the car, open the little gate at the end of the path and look up at the house. Such a pretty house, now filled with sadness. I've ruined their happy home. I knock gently on the door.

First I hear a dog trying to sniff me under the door. I cross my fingers and hope they're out. *Please be out, I'm not ready for this.* Then I hear footsteps. And then the door opens. Mrs Richardson is standing in front of me, and the world stops turning.

'Mrs Richardson, I don't know if you remember me. I'm R—'

'Renée? Renée Sargent?' she says, looking at me in a completely unreadable way. She goes still, then steps forward quickly and I think she's going to punch me, so I shut my eyes and hold my breath.

But she doesn't.

She hugs me.

Sitting alone on the sofa in the living room, I take in my surroundings. It isn't a sad room. It's full of photographs of Matt, his mum and a man I presume to be his dad. There is also a picture of Jesus over the fireplace, and a cross above the door. As I look closer I see a picture frame with some writing in it. It says:

May your Mother's Day be as beautiful as the Love in
  your Heart
THANKS for being such a wonderful mother
Matt x

I turn away from it quickly. I can't read things like that right
now. I can't handle it.

'You said no sugar, didn't you?'

'Yes.'

I take the tea.

'Thank you for coming. I'm sure you were very nervous,'
Mrs Richardson says, sitting next to me on the sofa. Her face
is puffy.

'I thought you would hate me, not want me here.'

'Hate you? I don't hate you, Renée. You were the last person
to see my son before he died. That makes you special to me,
special to him too. I can't hate you.'

My body adjusts to the relief. I hadn't realised how tense
every muscle in my body was until she said that.

'You seem OK,' I say. Knowing I worded it badly.

'I am so sad, Renée. Matt was an angel, my angel. My only
son, all I had left in the world.' A single tear runs down her
right cheek and I see that she is far from OK.

'What about Mr Richardson. How is he?'

'There is no Mr Richardson any more, I'm afraid. My husband
died when Matt was ten. It was just Matt and me.'

My eyes fill up with tears. Damn it! I don't want to cry in

front of her. It isn't fair. I have no right. She is the one who should cry, not me. I feel selfish and pathetic. How dare I come here and sob to the woman who just lost her son when all I have is a broken arm?

And then she puts her hand on my knee.

'Dear Lord,' she says. Her eyes are closed, and out of respect I close mine too. 'Please help Renée through this time. Help her see that there is no anger, no hate, and that she must enjoy being young, and live her life the way she always wanted. Please help her rest at night and free her mind of worry and guilt. Please forgive her as I have, Lord, and let her life be full of joy and happiness, and not let what has happened infringe upon her youth. Thank you, Lord. Amen.'

'Amen,' I say. But what I wanted to say was thank you.

We talk a little longer about what she has organised for the funeral. The choir Matt sang in when he was younger, a reading by his cousin. She has it all under control. I think she's incredible. When I've finished my tea, I say I had better go.

As I make my way to the front door, Mrs Richardson behind me, I turn back to her.

'Even if you don't think I should say it, I am so sorry for what's happened. I'll always think of Matt, and if it's OK with you, when I come back to Guernsey after I've left, I'll come and see you, just to make sure you are all right?'

'I'd love that, thank you.'

I open the front door and step out.

'And Renée?' says Mrs Richardson. 'I knew your mother. We were friends in school. I always loved her, so funny and energetic and beautiful. You look just like her.'

All at once all the feelings that have been churning around me the past few months seems to collide together and I throw myself at Mrs Richardson and squeeze her as hard as I can. I think of Matt and I hold her even tighter. I will never stop being grateful for her grace. Ever.

'I'm so proud of you,' says Aunty Jo as I get in the car.

'I'm proud of Matt's mum.' I wave to Mrs Richardson who is still at the door. 'Being so caring when she must feel like dying.' I shut my eyes, feeling a bit stronger now. I turn to my aunt. 'Please will you drop me off at Dean's?'

'Of course.' Aunty Jo pauses as if she has something else to say that she isn't sure about. 'I'm glad you're feeling more yourself . . . And actually I was wondering – and please say if this is not OK – but I was wondering if you would mind watching Nana tomorrow night. I'm . . . well, I've been asked out to dinner. I won't go if you would rather I didn't, but if you could, I . . . '

I smile at her. She looks so flustered. I've never seen her like this before.

'Sure. Anyone nice?'

'Yes,' she says sweetly. 'Very nice indeed.'

When I knock on his door he answers it so quickly I wonder if he was just sitting there waiting for me.

'Babe, you're here. I've missed you so much. Come in, come on. I'll take care of you.'

His cuddle is so nice. He is warm and loving and just the way I've always wanted him to be. I know he's always fancied me, but this affection is new. He wants to take care of me and it feels good. He leads me into the kitchen and puts the kettle on.

'Now, I want you to start from the beginning. Who was Matt? Was he a friend of yours?'

'Not really. I mean, I knew who he was, but I always thought he was a bit weird and desperate. I'd never really spoken to him before. But I'd fallen out with Flo, and Matt was there, and he and Flo . . . well, they had a bit in common, and I thought Matt would be able to help me sort things out with her so that's why I let him drive my car.'

He listens to me while making some tea. Telling me to slow down and explain properly. He is being so sweet. We go through into the lounge and he sits with me on the sofa.

'Your arm must be so sore. I'll have to be careful when I make love to you tonight.' He says it like he's joking, but I know he isn't.

'Dean . . . maybe not tonight, OK?'

'God, of course. I'm sorry. Of course it's OK, I can wait. So tell me more, what happened after the cars hit each other?'

I'm just registering the blunt inappropriateness of that question right now, when the front door opens and Meg walks into the flat.

'Renée, babe. How are you?' she says, sounding spaced as usual.

I can't believe it. Couldn't he have told her no, just for today? Just for once I want to be alone with Dean, but Meg is always here, everywhere I look. I don't want to be the moody girlfriend, but sometimes maybe girlfriends should be moody.

'Renée was just telling me all about the accident,' says Dean, like I've been talking about a film I went to see or something.

'Oh wow, don't let me stop you. Carry on,' says Meg. 'Sounds intense.'

Intense? I have no clue how to respond to this. Why do neither of them think this is weird?

'Actually, I don't want to talk about it any more. Sorry.'

'Meg, roll us a spliff, will you?' says Dean. 'Renée and I are going to chill in my room tonight.'

At least Dean gets it. Kind of. He wants us to be alone. He wants to take care of me.

That makes me feel so much better.

Lying on his bed I tell him everything. The way I was covered in Matt's blood, how I felt when I opened my eyes.

'His hand was on my leg,' I tell him. 'I saw it and it took me a while to remember whose it could be and where I was. Then I realised that the thing pressing against me was him.'

'It's so awful, babe.' He hugs me and I sob gently onto his chest. 'I'm here, I've got you now. Don't worry. Here, have some of this, it will help you sleep.' He passes me the joint and after a few puffs I do my usual wind-down and my eyes start drooping. I feel so safe in his arms, and like when this is all over we will be happy and maybe I will move in, and we will . . . we will . . . I feel myself falling into a peaceful sleep. It's nice. I haven't had a peaceful sleep in a while. Dean gently moves me off him and lays me down. He kisses my forehead softly and strokes my hair.

'You sleep,' he says. 'You sleep, I will come to bed soon.'

He shuts his bedroom door and I drift off.

I wake up and for a few blissful seconds I forget about the hideous events of the past week. Dean's bed is so comfy and soft and warm. It's dark, obviously not morning yet, and he isn't next to me. I look at the alarm clock. It's just gone ten o'clock. I have been asleep for hours. I get out of bed and go to the bathroom. Music is coming from the lounge but no voices. Dean must have told Meg to go home.

After a wee – I've got used to doing it with one hand now – I head for the lounge. I'm still very sleepy. When I open the door Dean's face is right in front me. He is kneeling on the floor with his hands on something. It takes me a moment to work out that it's Meg's bum. She is also on her knees but leaning forward in front of him. He's doing her from behind. It looks so casual, so unenergetic. It's so quiet and unpassionate, which is why I think I don't realise what is happening straight away.

'Babe!' he says, seeing me.

He pulls out of Meg and nudges her so she flops to the side and out of his way.

'Babe, I . . . ' Dean looks kind of sorry, but at the same time, like he couldn't care less. He is obviously off his face.

'So this is why you always come to bed later than me?'

'Babe . . . '

'Stop FUCKING saying babe. I'm not your babe. Have you got any idea what the last week has been like for me?'

He goes to hug me, but I don't let him. His penis is hanging out the bottom of his T-shirt. I don't want it anywhere near me. Urgh, it strikes me that this is why it always smells of soap in the mornings. Urgh. Urgh urgh urgh . . .

'You're a disgusting person,' I tell him, and I'm surprised at how calm I sound.

'Renée, don't overreact,' Dean says, and then he yawns loudly.

'Let's try to be grown-up about this, shall we?'

'Fuck off, Dean.' I turn my gaze to Meg. 'And what kind of cow are you?' I ask her.

Meg can barely open her eyes. Her body is completely floppy. She's totally wasted. She manages to hold her head up long enough to say, 'I'm just paying my rent, babe.'

'You are both disgusting.' I grab my bag from the floor. 'So disgusting. What was I thinking? Of course this was happening. You fuckers!'

I slam the front door behind me as I leave. I can just hear Dean shouting, 'Babe, babe!' He doesn't come after me, though. I don't even want him to.

Out on the street I don't know where to go. I have no car, and my arm is so sore. I'm still blurry from waking up. I don't have the energy to do anything. I see a phone box. I find a ten-pence piece in my bag. I manage to dial. I am so relieved when she answers.

'Please come and get me.'

Then I sit on the floor and wait.

Flo

'What did Dr Burrington say?' I ask Renée as she comes out of the doctor's.

'That it will take a few weeks for some of the results to come in and that if I have anything she will tell me when I call. It's so gross being tested. She basically put a giant metal hand up my vagina and cranked me open.'

196

'You mean she gave you a smear test?'

'Yeah, that. She gave me that and she took my wee and she scraped me with something else. I might never have sex again if that is what you have to do.'

'Or you could just use a condom and look after yourself a bit better?'

'All right, Virgin Face, all right.'

That's the first thing she's said that has sounded like the old her since the accident. Insulting as it is, it makes me happy.

'Shall we go to the Vazon caff, get chips and walk along the beach?' I ask her, knowing what the answer will be.

'I'd love that,' she says. 'I have to be home by six, though. Aunty Jo has a date.'

On the beach we sit against the wall, a portion of chips on each of our laps. It's so peaceful and beautiful.

'I'm going to miss Guernsey so much,' I say, wondering if Nottingham will be as pretty. 'How are you feeling about the exams next week? And I'm not hassling you, I just want to know. What with what's happened and the funeral and everything, I just want to know how you're feeling about it all. That's all.'

'It's OK, I know you never meant to hassle me. I don't want to fall out with you ever again.' Renée eats some chips. 'In all honesty I'm not thinking about them at all. I don't feel like my life depends on my A-level results. I don't want to go to uni so I don't need to do well. I don't need good grades to travel, do I?'

'You want to travel?'

'I think so, Flo. I think I'd like to be a food critic.'

197

'A food critic?' I can't help but laugh at how random that is.

'Aunty Jo says she knew a guy when she lived in London who just travelled the world writing about food. I could do that.'

Six months ago I would have told her to get her head out of the clouds, but the thing about Renée is that if she wants to be a food critic, she probably will be one. There's no point in trying to make someone like her do anything she doesn't want to do. And I don't point out that she might need to get some qualifications to be a food critic. The main thing is, she has an ambition.

'What about you?' she asks. 'Is God going with you when you leave?'

'Yes, I think he is. I know you think I'm nuts, but I feel happier and much more confident since I started going to church. It's been good for me. Changed me for the better. You just have to accept it.'

'I do. I mean, I'm always going to think you're a little bit mad, but I accept it. We don't have to believe in the same thing to be best friends, do we?'

'We really don't. Maybe it's a good thing. At least we'll never get bored.'

'I think I'm going to go to Spain as soon as the exams are finished,' says Renée. 'Aunty Jo suggested it, so I spoke to Nell and she wants me to go. Maybe it's time to see if I can get to know Dad a bit. This whole thing with Matt has made me think about family a lot more.'

'When will you come back?' I ask, trying not to sound selfishly upset that she won't spend the summer with me.

'For the results. I'll be gone a few months. You could come

out for a holiday?'

'Maybe. Mora has given me full-time work until I leave, though. I'm going to need all the money I can get when I go to university, so I'm going to try and save loads. I'll miss you. I can't imagine it.'

'I'll miss you too.'

We both stare out to sea. It seems impossible to make plans, to talk about the future we have no idea about. All we know is that the time has come and everything is going to change, and there is nothing we can do to stop it.

'I love you,' she tells me, looking at me and smiling.

'I love you too,' I say, resting my head on her good shoulder. 'I love you more than anyone in the world.'

9

Headlines

Renée

I barely slept last night because today is likely to be one of the worst days of my life. The funeral is at eleven o'clock at the town church, and I'm dreading it with every inch of my soul.

I've had little contact with anyone since the accident. Just family, Flo, Dr Burrington and obviously Dean and Meg, but I am trying not to think about those scumbags. I can't believe I was so stupid as to not see what was going on. What else could a weird relationship like that be about? The words 'Just paying my rent, babe' keep ringing in my head. It was all so skanky and grim, I feel riddled with them, and I am so happy that when I called Dr Burrington yesterday she told me my results were in early and that I've got away without any horrible STDs. At least that's one thing.

I feel like I'm learning big lessons very young, and I know over time I will get over those two. They'll pale into insignificance in my life, and I'll never be so stupid again, or so gullible. But that doesn't mean I am dealing with it very well at the moment. Along with the shock and sadness about Matt, I am just so embarrassed about how I let Dean and Meg make such a fool of me.

I look in my wardrobe for black clothes and see the outfit that Flo wore that first morning she went to church. It seems appropriate. If I had known that I would be wearing it for something like this, I might never have made fun of her that day.

I go downstairs and into the kitchen. Aunty Jo quickly grabs a newspaper and throws it under the kitchen table.

'What was that?' I ask.

'What? Nothing.'

'Yes, there was something. That newspaper, why did you just throw it under the table?'

'I did? Oh that, yes, I was just swatting a fly.'

'Don't lie to me,' I say, kneeling down to pick it up. 'You were hiding someth— THE ARSEHOLE!'

Eighteen-year-old Guernsey barmaid, Renée Sargent, involved in fatal car crash.

Written by Dean Mathews.

'Now, darling, stay calm,' says Aunty Jo, putting her hands out towards me like she is trying to tame a lion. 'People don't take any notice of this stuff. It's tomorrow's chip paper.'

I keep reading. Certain lines jump out at me and punch me in the face.

'I thought he was weird,' says Renée Sargent of Matt Richardson.

After a blazing row with a friend, Sargent instigated a

sick car game, putting herself and others in danger. The game went wrong when Sargent attempted to seduce Richardson, causing the young Christian to drive to his death.

I sit on the floor in the kitchen and sob.

'I can never leave the house again,' I blub.

Aunty Jo sits next to me. She takes the *Guernsey Globe* out of my hand and puts it under her bum so I can't see it.

'You have done everything right. Everything. Remember Mrs Richardson and how glad she was that you went to see her? Focus on that. Dean is bad news. He's trying to get noticed as a writer and doesn't care who he brings down along the way. You have a heart, he doesn't. Now let's get up. Flo will be here in a minute and we need to get going. You have to be strong, OK? For Matt.'

Every time I think I've hit my lowest point something happens to get me even lower. Maybe there is no lowest point. Maybe as humans we just go down and down and down until we die. I feel the same way I did before I jumped off the wall. Like I want to let fate decide if I will be OK or not, because I don't have the energy to make things better by myself. I can't be bothered to drag myself out of this heap I keep finding myself in. I'm exhausted with being me.

'Morning,' says Flo, walking into the kitchen in a black shirt and trousers. 'Are you ready?'

I pass her the newspaper. She starts to say the obvious angry thing but stops herself and says, 'Today we think about Matt, OK? We will deal with this tomorrow.'

The doorbell rings. Suddenly Mr Frankel is in my kitchen again. This is becoming normal.

'Off you go,' he says, ushering us all out of the door. 'Nana and I will be fine until you get back.'

I'm too confused about everything to question how bizarre it is that Mr Frankel is babysitting Nana. Aunty Jo, Flo and I get into the car.

The rats crawl back into my stomach.

Flo

Renée squeezes my hand tightly as we walk into the church.

'I'm scared,' she says into my ear as I lead her to an empty pew. We sit down.

'Don't be. Think of this as the nicest place in the world. Everyone is here to pay their respects to Matt. No one here is angry and no one will judge you.'

She looks so small and delicate. Mousey and afraid. So not like Renée. The church is filling up quickly, but she doesn't look up and watch people in her usual curious way. She keeps her head down, as if she's been told off.

'But I know what everyone is really thinking. They will all have seen Dean's article. They all think I'm the slut who killed him.'

I swallow the urge to ask her not to use words like 'slut' in church, but I'm sure God will forgive her loose tongue considering the circumstances.

'Renée, who cares if they do? We all know the truth, the

people who love you.'

'But I care what people think. I care a lot. They think that Mrs Richardson hates me. They don't know that I went to see her, that we talked.'

'Renée, remember, today is about Matt.'

We are about ten rows from the front, and Renée is between me and Aunty Jo. Matt's coffin is not far away. Renée hasn't looked at it once, but I can't take my eyes off it. Poor Matt. I still don't think it's hit me that he's dead. I know I have my own pain yet to come.

'Just keep your head down if it makes you feel better,' I tell Renée, noticing that some people are looking at her. I am worried that if she sees them she'll just run out. I can't imagine how self-conscious she feels, how responsible.

A few rows behind us I see Pete and Marcus with their parents. Both of them look destroyed. All of that cocky confidence is gone as they cry and stare at Matt's coffin in disbelief. Then I notice Mrs Richardson walk in. Head to toe in black and wearing a black hat with a black net that covers her face. She is with another lady who is similar to her in age and a man who is crying. Maybe an uncle of Matt's?

As they walk to the front of the church people pretend not to stare, but they all do. Some eyes flit between Mrs Richardson and Renée, hoping to sense some drama. Mrs Richardson walks past us slowly and Renée still doesn't look up. She walks directly to her son's coffin, puts her hand on it and prays. People begin to sob.

When she is done she turns and sees Renée. Rather than take her seat at the front, she slowly walks back up the aisle and stops at our pew. Everyone is prepared for an outburst. Aunty Jo and I look at each other, worried that maybe her attitude has changed.

Then Mrs Richardson leans forward and raises Renée's chin with her finger.

'Come and sit with me at the front. Please?' she says gently. And to the amazement of everyone in the church, Renée, hand in hand with Matt's mother, goes to sit at the front with the small amount of family present. I'm not sure I have ever witnessed anything so magical.

The service is lovely. Matt is described perfectly by the vicar as 'sweet, kind and loving'. The vicar even asks everyone to pray for Renée, which will hopefully be the end of any judgement from anyone else. Gordon sings a song on his guitar and of course chooses one that has the words Christ, Jesus or God in every line. We try to avoid each other but make accidental eye contact as he finishes his song. I give him a little smile, and he gives me one back. We are different people, and it's not to be, but that's OK. This is no place to bear a grudge.

At the end of the service there is the feeling that everyone in the church has experienced something spiritual together. Even the atheists amongst us must have felt it. I don't see one single person without tears running down their face.

The family leave first and as Mrs Richardson and Renée reach us, Renée holds out her hand and I take it. I walk out with her. As we step out into Town Square the daylight makes our sore, red eyes squint, and as things come into focus, we gasp. As far as we can see up the high street there are people. Hundreds and hundreds of them who couldn't fit into the church but wanted to pay their respects. Mrs Richardson closes her eyes and inhales, as if taking in all of their love. It's breathtaking.

'He would have loved this,' I say to Renée. 'All he ever wanted was to be accepted and popular, and look at that. He got what he always wanted.'

'I've never seen anything like it,' says Renée, obviously feeling a little more confident than before the service.

Aunty Jo and I walk her slowly to the car.

August 1997

10

Time Goes By

Renée

'Look at you and your suntan! You look so well,' says Aunty Jo when she picks me up from the airport. 'That trip did you the world of good!'

It really did. Getting through the exams was torture. School felt so dark, so depressed. Every time I walked in or out I had to see the lay-by and all the memories of that horrible day came flooding back to me. It was the most twisted and difficult time of my entire life. I resented having to go back to that building and I felt like everyone was talking about me all the time. Matt's ghost followed me everywhere for the few weeks after the funeral. No matter how supportive people were I couldn't escape the facts of what happened. I threw him my keys and let him drive my car, and he died because I did that. It will always be something I battle with, but I know now that over time I'm going to be able to build my life around it. I've learned a lot about who I want to be, and being good to the people I love is top of my agenda. I've not worked hard enough on that in the past, taking people for granted and always putting myself first. It isn't OK for me to be like that any more. I'm going to take better care of everyone from now on, and do my best not to let anybody down. I'll be a better person.

Spain was really good for me. I was so nervous when I arrived, nervous to see Dad for the first time in ten years, nervous to see Nell and to meet my step-mum and two little half-brothers. But as soon as I arrived it just worked. Sure, Dad and I had some work to do on our relationship. I felt angry with him at first, but then me, Dad and Nell talked a bit, and I realised how Nana and Pop – but mostly Pop – had made it so hard for Dad to be a part of our lives. I also realised how much Mum dying had broken him and that Guernsey was too painful a place to be. He never should have left me and Nell. I am not sure I will ever understand why he wouldn't take us with him, but I'm beginning to learn that being an adult is hard work and full of tough decisions, and that you don't always make the right ones. The most important thing is that you learn from your mistakes, and make up for them as best you can when you get the chance.

Dad was really trying to make it up to me. To get to know me and make me a part of his life. His wife, Maria, is lovely too. A large Spanish motherly type who just wants to take care of everybody. I'd spoken to her on the phone before, and she's always sent me birthday and Christmas cards since she's been with Dad, so I had no real reason not to like her. She was funny and kind and a really good cook. She made huge Spanish dinners, which even Nell ate.

Their house is so pretty, just outside a small village in Andalusia. There are vineyards and in the village there are lots of cafés and bars. I worked in one of them and have actually managed to save quite a bit of money.

I feel a bit better about everything that happened. Mrs Richardson and I have spoken on the phone a few times and I sent her postcards all the time. Aunty Jo brought Nana out for a holiday, which was funny because she really didn't have a clue where she was. She kept thinking Aunty Jo had redecorated and that was why the house looked different. I was so happy when everyone was together, I couldn't believe it was my family.

Nell and I got on OK too. We had to share a room again, but this time around it wasn't so bad. I'm really glad she moved out there when she did. At the time it broke my heart, but I've never seen her so happy. And she's put on a bit of weight. She's still a bit weird about food. I think she always will be. But all she wanted was to be with her dad, and I'm happy she's got him to look after her now.

I definitely want to go back to Spain next month to work. Maria says she knows someone at the local English-speaking paper for all the ex-pats, so I'm going to go and see them and see if I can get some work experience, and start writing food reviews and see if they will print any. I might as well try. All in all I'm feeling really positive about life again, but I really missed Flo.

'Is it all right if I go and stay with Flo tonight?' I ask Aunty Jo. 'Then we can go to school together tomorrow and get our results.'

'Of course. Why don't you come home, see Nana, drop off your bags and then I'll drive you round. There is something I need to tell you when we get there too.'

'Who is with Nana now?' I ask her, knowing she won't have left her alone.

'That's what I need to talk to you about.'

As we pull up to the house there is a car in the driveway. It looks familiar, but I can't place whose it is. Aunty Jo has gone a bit quiet. She has a cheeky look on her face, like she has done something naughty. In the house there is a man's jacket hanging on the stairs, and a pair of familiar-looking glasses by the phone. Surely not?

'Hello, Renée. Welcome home,' says Mr Frankel, coming out of the kitchen.

'Mr Frankel, what, are you . . . ?' I start to put the pieces together. 'Wait, are you two . . . ?'

'You're going to have to get used to calling me James,' he says, walking past me to Aunty Jo so he can put his arm around her.

'James?' I say 'Uncle James?' We all laugh. These two getting together is the best thing I have ever seen. 'I LOVE this!' I tell them, hugging them both. 'I love this SO much!'

'And we're not the only ones. Come and see this,' says Aunty Jo, leading me outside. 'Look at Freddie.'

I look at our goose in his little enclosure, proud as anything with his head held high, sitting next to Feathers. He looks like his old self again.

'Where's Flapper?' I ask.

'We had to get her a new home. It just wasn't going to work having the three of them. She was so left out. Freddie took a shine to Feathers, the two of them paired off and poor Flapper was left on her own all the time. It was sad to see. As soon as she left these two were so happy. He's the best he's ever been, completely in love.'

We watch them for a few minutes. It's very sweet.

'Please can I go and see Flo now?' I ask, not able to wait any longer. I haven't told her I'm back and want to surprise her.

'Here, I'll take you,' says Mr Fra— James.

'You won't try to make me read Chaucer on the way, will you?' I joke.

'Renée, it was hard enough to get you to read anything while you were at school!' he says back, grabbing his keys.

Flo

I'm so nervous about the results. I know there is nothing I can do about it now, and what will be will be, but the fear that I won't have passed and that I won't get to go where I want to go is worrying me. Tomorrow is D-Day. I will know. I need an A and two Bs. What with everything that was going on while we were doing the exams, and having to look after Renée, I just don't know how I've done.

There is a knock at the door.

'Flo, can you get that? Arthur and I are putting shelves up in the bedroom.' shouts Mum. They've been busy all day making changes to the bedroom because Arthur is moving in.

I reluctantly get off my bed and go downstairs. I hope it's not Sandra. She keeps coming round with snacks.

I open the door.

'*Hola*,' says Renée, looking beautiful with a huge smile and a suntan. I'm so happy to see her I squeak.

'God, I've missed you so much!' I say, latching onto her like a limpet. 'You didn't tell me you were coming back today!'

'Ooo, my arm, my arm. It's still not quite healed,' says Renée. I let go of her and press my cheek against hers. I just want to be as close to her as possible. 'Of course I am back, it's results day tomorrow.'

'I didn't think you would care about the results. I thought maybe Aunty Jo would get them for you. I'm so glad you came. I've missed you so much. I can't be in Guernsey without you.'

'I'm here now, and I am with you until you go.'

'If I go. I have to pass first.'

'Flo, you pass everything. There is no way you won't get the grades you want. Now, can I come in?'

We head to the kitchen and pile cheese and crackers and all sorts of other things on plates and take them up to my room. In bed, head to toe, we tell each other everything about our summers, and chat into the night until we fall asleep.

'I can't,' I say.

'Yes, you can, Flo. Come on,' Renée insists.

'I can't.'

'Flo, get in the car. We are going.'

'But what if I've failed. I don't want to know.'

'You won't have failed. You never fail anything at school.

Get in and drive.'

I do as she says and start the engine. I drive us to school really slowly, hoping for a puncture the whole way so I can put it off.

'Park as close to the entrance as you can, I don't want to be near the lay-by,' Renée says. I can't imagine what it must be like for her coming back here.

Luckily the car park is almost empty as it's the holidays. I get us as close as I can.

'Right, let's do this,' she says. 'Not that I care.'

We walk up the steps and into the main entrance of the school. People from our year are all around us and most of them look quite happy with themselves. It's so weird to think my future depends on what is inside the envelope. We get to the canteen and see the table with the results on. Renée walks ahead and gets ours.

'Here you go,' she says, returning and passing me mine.

I start to gently peel open the envelope. You'd think there was a dead body in it the way I'm acting. I feel so terrified. This is it, school over forever. Done. The results in this envelope tell me if I made the most of it or not, or if the whole thing has been a waste of time.

'Oh for God's sake, Flo,' says Renée, snatching it out of my hand. 'Stop being such a wuss.' She rips open my envelope and hands it back to me.

'There, you moron, you did it. Look, you passed! An A and two Bs. You're in!'

I look at the paper. She's right. Oh my God, she's right. I scream and jump up and down and hug her, but she tells me to get off because of her arm.

'I did it!' I keep saying. 'I did it!'

'My turn. Not that it matters. I don't need good grades. It means nothing to me.'

She opens her envelope and a huge smile appears across her face.

'What, you passed them all?'

'No. I got an E for Classics, an N for Home Ec, but a B for English. That's the best I've ever done in anything. B in English? Me?'

She looks so happy. It turns out it really did matter after all.

'Flo,' calls someone behind me. It's Kerry. She looks happy. 'How did you do?'

'I passed, I got what I needed. I can't believe it,' I tell her.

'Me too. Well done.'

'Thanks.'

There are a few seconds of awkward silence. I think Kerry is hoping Renée will step away. But of course she doesn't.

'Look,' Kerry says anyway. 'I'm really sorry if I embarrassed you when I told you I thought you were gay. I just . . .'

Renée makes a very strange croaking noise as she half laughs and half chokes.

I have gone a ripe beetroot colour.

'Kerry, don't worry about it. I just hope we can be friends and put it all behind us,' I say, avoiding Renée's eyes, which are like lasers in the side of my head. She will laugh her head off when I tell her about all of this.

'What's this then? A lesbian convention?' It's Bernadette. She obviously has no intention of stopping bullying Kerry, even though school is over. 'Are your grades good enough to go to the school of massive lesbians together now?' She laughs, and her two disciples laugh loyally.

'What did you say?' says Renée.

Uh-oh. An unsuspecting Bernadette hasn't met Renée when she's sticking up for me yet.

'I said are these two lezzers going –'

'Yeah, I heard what you said. Do you know what I think?'

'What?' says Bernadette, not enjoying being stopped in her tracks.

'I think you should go and pick on someone your own size, like a man?'

We all watch as Bernadette's ego pours into the ground.

'So take your massive shoulders and your big face and fuck off, OK?' finishes Renée, shooing Bernadette away like an annoying fly. 'Go on, off you pop.'

Bernadette turns slowly and walks away. She doesn't even try to come back to what Renée said – what could you possibly say to that? All we hear as she walks away is her telling her two stooges to shut up, because neither of them can stop laughing.

'Thanks,' says Kerry. 'It looks like you have your best friend back, Flo. Maybe see you in church soon?'

'Sure,' I say, giving her a hug.

Kerry walks away, and it takes Renée all of four seconds to laugh so hard she is almost sick.

'You? A lesbian? Jesus. You're terrified of your own vagina, how would you cope with someone else's?'

Yup, my best friend is back, all right.

Renée

I guess I didn't realise how important it was for me to pass English. But then I never missed a lesson and I did all of my coursework. I'm so chuffed that I got a B. Apart from anything else, now that Mr Frankel is practically related to me it makes going home a lot less awkward.

As we leave the school I see Emma Morton going in, looking much healthier. She smiles at me as she walks past and I smile back. I'm happy to see she managed to sit the exams. I hope she gets what she wants.

And then I see Meg.

She's leaving with her envelope and walking up the road and away from town, which means she isn't going to Dean's. Where is she going? Pissed off with her as I am, I'm still fascinated to know what she's all about. I'm going to follow her.

'Flo, do you mind if I walk home? I could do with some air.'

'No, I was going to just drop you home anyway. There's someone I have to go and see. See you tonight for some celebratory drinks?'

'Definitely. And Flo? Well done, I'm so proud of you.'

'I'm proud of you too,' she beams. 'See you later.'

I run out of the car park and follow the road that Meg is walking along, being careful not to get too close so that she senses me. I don't know where she lives, but it can't be far if she's walking.

I was wrong. We walk for nearly half an hour. Eventually she turns into an estate not far from Cobo Bay and goes into a house. It's one of those houses that looks like all the other

218

ones on the street. Boring but nice. I don't see anything about it that would be so hideous she wouldn't want to stay there and instead sleep on a couch with a thin blanket. But I guess I know the real reasons she slept at Dean's now. Although it still doesn't make any sense.

I don't know why I followed her. What am I hoping to see? As I think about leaving I wonder how much better I will feel if I confront her. If I just knock on the door and ask her why she treated me that way, and tell her how she made me feel. People like Meg should know the damage they do or they'll just keep on doing it. She made me look like a fool and humiliated me night after night. She shouldn't get away with it. So after half an hour of hiding in a bush outside her house, I go and knock on the door. After two long minutes, she opens it. She's wearing a T-shirt and just her knickers. Like I've seen her so many times before.

'Renée? What are you doing here?'

'I followed you from school. I wasn't going to knock, but I think you need to know how you made me feel. You really hurt me, sleeping with Dean. I thought he was my boyfriend.'

'There are about five girls right now who think they're Dean's girlfriend. Dean doesn't do girlfriends, Renée.'

He was seeing more people? How could I have been so stupid? It all seems so obvious now.

'And so what are you? What makes you different?'

'Renée, it's complicated and I really want you to leave if that's . . .'

A male voice comes from upstairs.

'Megan! Where's my fucking whisky? Have you hidden

my whisky?'

Meg looks nervous.

'Please, Renée, you should leave.'

'Who is that?' I ask her. 'Is that your dad?'

She doesn't answer and I roll my eyes.

'Meg, Dean is using you for sex. He used me and he obviously uses other people too . . . '

'Look, Renée, Dean lets me stay, OK? I give him what he wants and he gives me somewhere to stay when I need it. My part of the deal is as good as his, OK? Do you understand?'

The man's voice comes again. This time it's louder.

'Meg! Get inside, you lazy little tart.'

My mouth drops open. Is Meg's dad really talking to her like that?

'Please, just go.' Meg looks actually upset for the first time ever.

'Are you OK?' I ask her. No wonder she never wants to stay here, I think.

Meg shakes her head, like she's warning me off.

'Are you s—' I try again.

'Renée, just go home,' she says. 'Seriously.'

'Fine, OK, I'll go.' I shrug and turn away from her.

But before she closes the door she calls after me, 'Renée?'

I turn back to her.

'Don't think too badly of me, OK? Please?'

'I won't,' I say, meaning it.

She shuts the door.

Flo

I feel like everything is coming together. Mum's found Arthur, Renée knows she wants to go back to Spain, I got the grades I need to go to uni. Life is shifting into place. I've changed so much as a person this year. I'm more comfortable in myself than I've ever been, I know who I am better than ever before. Church has helped me with that. I'll always be insecure, but that's OK – I think everyone probably is.

I don't think I am into religious rock groups, and even weekly Bible meetings might be a bit too much, but I've found something this summer, something that held me up when I was about to fall. I think my faith is here to stay. The church gives me a place to be neutral, to feel like the things that stress me out are manageable. It's given me a way of coping, it's guided me through another tough period in my life. I just wish I had found it sooner. It's taught me how to trust in myself, and it's taught me how to forgive. How to really forgive, and that's why I'm about to do what I'm about to do. I am going to turn over the final stone that will truly release me into the next stage of my life. My final challenge.

I knock on the door. It opens.

'Flo, what are you doing here?'

'Hello, Sally.'

'Excuse the mess,' Sally says, bending down in front of me to pick up some kids' toys. Her bottom eclipses the floor, she's put on so much weight. She was always so skinny. Being bigger doesn't suit her.

'I'd make you some tea but I've been in the kitchen for the last hour washing bottles and I can't be bothered to go back in.'

'Don't worry. I'm fine. So how have you been?' I ask.

'OK. Being a mum isn't as easy as it looks, but it's all right. It didn't help that my dad cut me off.' She looks at me suspiciously. 'Not being funny, Flo, but what are you doing here?'

I see she hasn't lost her ability to be rude to me, even after two years.

'It was results day today. I passed everything and got what I need to go to uni.'

'Results day? Wow, I feel so out of touch with anything like that. I tried to stay at school, but I had a hard pregnancy. I was really sick and had every complication you could ask for. School became more hassle than it was worth, so I left. You going to go away then?'

'Yes, Nottingham,' I say. 'I'm excited. Look, I just wanted to come and see you because . . . our friendship really affected my life, Sally.'

'Well, we were friends for a long time, until you dumped me.'

I bite my tongue.

'You bullied me, Sally, for years. And I just wanted to say –'

There is a scream from upstairs. Her baby has woken up. As if I'm not even there she leaves the room and goes up to him. I follow the sound of his screams and find her in a tiny kids' bedroom bobbing him up and down. I carry on.

'You bullied me. I know you don't think you did, but you did.'

The screams are getting louder. But I don't stop.

'Every day you'd tell me I was rubbish. You thought I was ugly, stupid, unfunny. And I believed you.'

222

The wailing is out of control. As if the baby is responding to what I am saying, but she isn't.

'I'll always question myself because of the way you treated me. I don't think it will ever really go away. The sound of your voice belittling me, your jibes, the way you bossed me about.'

'Sorry, Flo. I think he has wind.'

The baby screams into her ear and I know what I am saying doesn't reach her, but I have to say it.

'But I forgive you, Sally. I forgive you for what you did to me for all of those years. And I'm going to get on with my life now, and do my best to move on from you.

'Sorry, what? Flo, just wait, I'll get him off again soon. Good boy, come on now, stop that noise.'

'Bye, Sally.'

She doesn't even notice me leaving.

11

Goodbye

Flo

'Don't turn my bedroom into a study when I've gone,' I say to Mum as she sits on my bed watching me pack my last few bits and bobs.

'Of course I won't. It's your room.'

'And don't redecorate. I like my wallpaper.'

'As if I have the time to redecorate,' she says huffily.

I sit on my case to shut it and look up at her as if to suggest that she help me, and then I see that she looks sad.

'Mum? What's the matter?'

'I'll miss you,' she says. 'I'll miss having you around.'

I don't know what to do with myself. In my entire life my mother has never said anything affectionate to me, or even suggested that she enjoyed my company. Even at our best, which has been over the last couple of years, there's been no hint of love.

'I know it's never been easy between us, Flo, but you are my daughter and I love you. I'm sorry I've not been such a great mother to you. I'm trying to make sure I don't mess Abi up in the same way.'

'Mum, I . . . '

'It's OK, you don't need to say anything, I don't blame you for hating me. Just come back and visit in the holidays, won't you? You will come back?'

'Of course I'll come back. This is my home. And I don't hate you, Mum.'

The strange thing is that I did hate her, for years. I hated her so much I wanted to hit her. But I don't now. And I don't want to leave with her thinking that I do.

'Maybe without me living here, we will be better friends,' I say.

'I'd like that,' she says. 'For us to be better friends.'

'I'd like that too.'

I zip up the last inch of my case.

'Wow, I couldn't have got another thing in. We should probably get going if we're going to have time to pick Renée up on the way to the airport. Is that still OK?'

'Of course. Flo . . .' Mum hesitates. I sense it would be inappropriate for me to move. 'I'm proud of you, Flo, for doing so well and getting into university. And your father would be too.'

This is where I crumble. Dad should be here to shut my suitcase and carry it to the car. I sit on it and drop my head as tears fall onto my legs. 'He should be here,' I say, looking up.

'Yes, he should. Come here,' says Mum. 'Come to me.' I go over to the bed to sit next to her, and we cuddle for the first time in about thirteen years.

Having picked up Renée, the two of us sit in the back with Abi in between us. Mum is driving and Arthur is in the passenger seat. We arrive at the airport and no one is saying anything.

'This is it,' says Arthur, breaking the silence.

We all get out of the car. Arthur goes to the boot to get my case. It's what Dad would have done.

'Let's say goodbye here,' says Mum. 'I can't stand farewells at airports.'

She is actually crying. I go to her and hug her and she kisses my face and then she pushes me away, but I know she doesn't mean to be cruel.

I kneel down to Abi.

'I'll miss you,' I say, kissing her head. 'You're the best little sister in the world and I'll be back soon. We can talk on the phone every day, OK? I'm not far away.'

She hugs me. She'll change so much by the time I see her next. I try not to think about that.

'I love you,' she tells me gently in my ear. I kiss her cheeks that are wet with tears.

'Bye, Arthur,' I say, kissing his cheek. 'Look after Mum for me, won't you?'

'Of course,' he says, and I know he will. He's the only man that's made her happy in years.

'You take her in, Renée,' says Mum. 'We'll wait for you and take you home when you're done.'

After checking in, Renée and I stand at the start of departures and laugh at how much we're crying.

'This is ridiculous,' she says. 'I can come and see you anytime.'

'Exactly. And I'll come to Spain. I can sit at the end of the bar you work in and you can sneak me drinks.'

'Yes, yes, we can do that.'

But although we know this isn't the end, it's scary.

'You're not to make any friends, OK, Flo? No one. You must be on your own at all times.'

'Got it. Just me and Jesus.'

'Yup, Jesus and me. We're your only friends. If someone tries to make conversation with you, you say no, I have enough friends. Go away. OK?'

We laugh and cry all at once.

'Will you be all right?' I ask her.

'I'll be fine. I'll go to Spain, get myself a hot Spanish boyfriend. I'll write restaurant reviews and work on my tan. It will be great.'

'It will.'

A voice comes over the Tannoy. *This is the last call for flight FB 4653 to East Midlands.*

'I'll miss you every day,' I say. 'You're my best friend in the world.'

She thinks for a second, then says, 'I'm your goose.'

'My goose?'

'Yeah, the one person you can always rely on – your goose.'

I don't know what she's talking about, but that's nothing new.

'I'd better go,' I say as we squeeze each other so hard my arm hurts. 'I love you.'

'I love you too. Don't go, Flo.'

'I have to. We have to live our lives, remember?'

I start to walk away. We're crying like we're never going to see each other ever again. As I get to the electric doors that take me through, I turn back and wave. As much as I tell myself I will see her soon, I can't help but doubt it as the doors close behind me.

No matter what happens from here, our lives will never be the same again.

Thanks to . . .

Everyone at Hot Key Books. Thank you for being brilliant to work with, for the encouragement and the support. You are the best bunch of people and you make me feel like I can write anything. It's a pleasure working with you.

Thanks to Adrian Sington for answering my calls, and Buzz for coping with me being a Moody Myrtle after long days and deadline panic sessions.

Thank you to Andrew Anthonio for being my constant security blanket and dear friend.

John de Garis for the cover photo, and my very own Renée and Flo, Elise and Kerry, for modelling for me again.

Thanks to Kate Earl, Louise Fletcher, Janet Unit and Sinead Wheadon for reminding me of how appalling my behaviour was during our A-levels and helping remember how it was to be an eighteen-year-old girl on Guernsey. Drunk, basically.

Thanks to my aunt and uncle for having geese and a beautiful home that I could call upon for inspiration. Thanks to my dad for letting me moan about my workload on the phone and my sister for doing the same.

Thanks to Eleanor Bergstein for the brilliant chats and best advice.

Thanks to everyone who read *Paper Aeroplanes*, and for all the feedback, good and bad.

Thanks to my husband for coping with my procrastinations and laughing at my jokes, and my BFFs Louise and Carrie for the constant inspiration. Both of you will see your influence in this book; I hope it makes you laugh.

And even though I have never met him, I should probably thank God.

Dawn O'Porter

Dawn O'Porter is a broadcaster, novelist and print journalist who lives in Los Angeles with her husband Chris, cat Lilu and dog Potato. She has made numerous documentaries about all sorts of things, including polygamy, childbirth, geisha, body image, breast cancer and even the movie *Dirty Dancing*. Dawn is currently the columnist for *Glamour* magazine in the UK, and writes regularly for many other publications. Her first novel, PAPER AEROPLANES, was published by Hot Key Books in 2013, to critical acclaim. GOOSE is the sequel and there are another two in the series yet to be written. She is also a highly prolific Tweeter (@hotpatooties) and manages her own website www.dawnoporter.co.uk.

Dawn is obsessed with vintage clothing and can be seen in *This Old Thing* on Channel 4, trying to convert high streetaholics to the way of old threads. Dawn also has her own clothing label called BOB (she also has a bob).

HOT KEY BOOKS

Thank you for choosing a Hot Key book.

If you want to know more about our authors
and what we publish, you can find us online.

You can start at our website

www.hotkeybooks.com

And you can also find us on:

We hope to see you soon!